ROCK'S HIDDEN PERSUADER:
THE TRUTH ABOUT BACKMASKING

ROCK'S
HIDDEN
PERSUADER:
THE TRUTH ABOUT
BACKMASKING

DAN & STEVE PETERS
WITH CHER MERRILL

BETHANY HOUSE PUBLISHERS

MINNEAPOLIS, MINNESOTA 55438
A Division of Bethany Fellowship, Inc.

Library of Congress Catalog Card Number 85–71475

ISBN 0–87123–857–8

Published by Bethany House Publishers
A Division of Bethany Fellowship, Inc.
6820 Auto Club Road, Minneapolis, Minnesota 55438

Printed in the United States of America

The Authors

DAN and STEVE PETERS are both ordained ministers and sons of a minister. They held their first rock music seminar in 1979 and since then have presented it scores of times in over 35 states. The bestselling *Why Knock Rock* was developed out of the seminars and has received a wide hearing. They live with their families in St. Paul, Minnesota.

CHER MERRILL, a free-lance writer who also lives in Minnesota, has worked closely with the Peters brothers in researching, developing and writing this material.

Contents

Introduction

The Subject Is Subliminals

"Say, say, say what you want/But don't play games with my affections." So goes the 1983–84 hit by Michael Jackson and Paul McCartney. Even the legendary superstars of rock music want people to "tell it like it is." No hidden agendas, no secret messages, no sham, no deception. And yet, one of the most controversial elements in the rock music industry has been the issue of subliminal messages hidden within the music—in other words, deception.

What is backmasking? Does it truly exist? Can subliminals actually affect the listener? Who is going to the trouble of concealing those inside-out missives on records? And the bottom line: Should a person be concerned?

In the early seventies accusations were hurled at certain rock groups, alleging they had laid subliminal messages on recording tracks in hopes of influencing listeners to take drugs, or worship Satan, or simply to buy more records. The technique, sometimes called "backmasking," has been fairly well documented on albums by such artists as the Beatles, the Rolling Stones and Pink Floyd.

Though the Peters brothers are much more uneasy about *audible, straightforward* messages than any covert communication on rock and roll recordings, and though we do not want people running out and buying records simply to check out the examples of substimuli we'll list later, the Bible does warn we should beware that Satan not take advantage of us (1 Pet. 5:8). Therefore, some investigation of the issue seems prudent.

The subject is a puzzling one, overshadowed with controversy. Hard, tested answers to the questions backmasking poses are as hidden as the subliminals themselves. With those qualifiers in mind, let's take a closer look at the subject of subliminals and see if we can discover the truth about rock's hidden persuaders.

1

Big Brother Eats Popcorn
The History of Sneaky Stimuli

In 1956, one of the first attempts at subconscious mind control in the Western world was organized by James Vicary and his Subliminal Projection Company. After applying for patents, Vicary sought out clients for a device that would flash on a movie screen, every five seconds for just 1/3000th of a second, a message such as, "Hungry? Eat Popcorn!" or "Drink Coca-Cola!"[1]

A Fort Lee, New Jersey, theater employed the device during a six weeks' screening of the film *Picnic*, and sales increased dramatically—popcorn by 57.5 percent and Coke sales by 18 percent,[2] but the theater refused to release any further details of the experiment.

The next year, the Precon Process and

---

[1]"Secret Voices," *Time* magazine (September 10, 1979), p. 71.
[2]R.C. Morse and David Stoller, "The Hidden Message That Breaks Habits," *Science Digest* (September 1982), p. 28.

Equipment Corporation was formed. Their stated purpose was to place subliminal messages in movies and taverns, and on billboards. The officers of the company included a psychologist, and a neurologist with engineering training. They claimed to have doubled, by subliminal methods only, the consumption of a beverage advertised on location. They later applied for and received a patent.[3] (The issuance of a patent does not necessarily guarantee that the device works efficiently, but Robert Richardson, primary examiner of the U.S. Patent and Trademark Office, has explained that if the patent office believes an invention cannot work, the application is not accepted.)[4]

The first known U.S. television broadcast of subliminals came the same year, says Dr. John Kamp, assistant to the Deputy Chief of the Mass Media Bureau in the Federal Communications Commission. It was then that station WTWO, in Bangor, Maine, tested the success of the technique by monitoring the reaction of viewers to flashes that stated, "If you have seen this message, write WTWO."

The station reported no increase in incoming mail, but that didn't dampen enthusiasm for the subliminal experimentation. During a five-week

---

[3]Vance Packard, *The People Shapers* (Boston: Little, Brown & Company, 1977), p. 135.
[4]Art Athens, "Beware Here Come the Mind Manipulators," *Family Health* magazine (December 1978), p. 40.

period in the spring of 1958, according to an FCC Information Bulletin, two researchers conducted an experiment on television station WTTV, Bloomington, Indiana.

In that video test, viewers were subliminally told to "Watch Frank Edwards," a news analyst featured on the station. The researchers reported once again, however, that the secret promotion had no "statistically significant effect" ("Televised Test of Subliminal Persuasion," *Public Opinion Quarterly*, Vol. 23, No. 2, pp. 168–180).

"In 1957, early into the period of experimentation," says Kamp, "the FCC published a notice expressing its concern. [The Commission] noted that subliminal messages only had been used by broadcasters for experimental purposes."

Unfortunately, the radio industry cannot claim the same innocent motives since it was also in 1957 that people discovered a Chicago-based (WAAF) radio station had been selling subliminal advertising space at $1,000 for 400 messages aired over a four-month period. Here also, results unfortunately were never made public.[5]

More audio versions of such subliminal information were reportedly tried by stations WCCO in Minneapolis, Minnesota; KLTI, Longview, Texas; KOL, Seattle, Washington; and KYA

---

[5]Packard, loc. cit. p. 135.

in San Francisco, California. These so-called "added recall devices" were messages prerecorded by disc jockeys and faded in under musical recordings or dropped into pauses in their dialogue in quick, low voices. Though these whispered quickie announcements could actually be heard by an intent listener, theoretically, the messages could be picked up on the subconscious level as well.

Other subliminal message experiments were attempted from the 1950's to the early 1970's. In the United States, network television companies, university professors and industrial scientists tested the silent seducers; and abroad, experiments were done by the British Broadcasting Corporation as well as other interested groups.

Del Hawkins, a professor of marketing at Southern Illinois University, conducted one such study in 1970. Entitled "The Effects of Subliminal Stimulation on Drive Level and Brand Preference," it was reported in *The Journal of Marketing Research* (August 1970).

Tests of 96 people who were given subliminal messages indicated that "a simple subliminal stimulus can serve to arouse a basic drive such as thirst."[6] The scientist also found that a person needs to be somewhat motivated for subliminals to work their best. In other words, you must be

---

[6]Del Hawkins, "The Effects of Subliminal Stimulation on Drive Level and Brand Preference," *The Journal of Marketing Research* (August 1970), p. 322.

vaguely hungry for an "Eat popcorn!" command to work.

Dr. Becker's Handy, Dandy Tachistoscope

Also in the late fifties, a Louisiana researcher in medical electronics, Dr. Hal C. Becker, was developing a device called a tachistoscope. Becker, who received his education from such notable universities as Tulane, MIT, Princeton, and George Washington University, has held a distinguished position on the staff at Tulane University Medical School for over 27 years. He is a specialist in bio-medical communication and clinical-behavioral engineering, and has received approximately $1,000,000 in research funds while publishing over 40 papers in scientific journals.[7]

The scientist-turned-subliminal-expert says he planned originally to use his device for flashing subliminal public service announcements, such as "drive safely," during television shows.[8]

The machine, which flashed images at 3- to 10-second intervals, was capable of introducing messages to the brain without the recipient's awareness. His work, and that of other researchers, essentially went underground, however, in the wake of public outcry.

---

[7]Wilson Bryan Key, *Clam Plate Orgy* (New Jersey: Prentice-Hall, Inc., 1980), p. 98.
[8]Morse and Stoller, loc. cit.

New Yorker magazine first blew the whistle on the secret messages, claiming "minds were being broken and entered." *Newsday* also picked up the battle cry, calling subliminals "the most alarming invention since the atomic bomb."[9]

Consequently, the fear of subconscious influence quickly brought about the production of laws in a number of countries around the world. Belgium defined subliminal technology as an invasion of privacy, in 1972, with penalties of up to one year in prison and fines of up to ten thousand francs.

This law applies to "anyone who by any means whatever projects images or sensations capable of influencing behavior whether or not consciously perceived."[10] Likewise, Great Britain has banned the use of subliminals.[11]

Surprisingly, however, although a number of legislators in the United States initially jumped on the bandwagon, and introduced a rash of bills, no laws were passed. And though the Federal Communications Commission did express "deep concern" over the use of subliminals on radio, the concern never became deep enough for them to actually formulate specific regulations. When the FCC was asked why not, they said subliminals would fall under the jurisdiction of the Federal Trade Commission, not the FCC.

---

[9]Packard, op. cit. p. 136.
[10]Key, op. cit. p. 144.
[11]Packard, op. cit. p. 137.

Bruce Parker, a lawyer for the FTC, refused to allow his organization to accept the burden, however. In 1980, he issued a statement that "subliminal technique is not specifically covered under any federal or state law."[12]

Obviously, a good deal of buck-passing has gone on with this issue. Only the National Association of Broadcasters has seen fit to respond to the demand. It issued a rule forbidding its members' use of subliminals. It was, at best, a watered-down effort; but it stemmed the tide of public demands, and talk of subliminal technology disappeared from the news. By 1970, the whole issue seemed quite dead.

Gone but Not Forgotten

In 1967, Alan Westin, a political scientist, speculated that if the 1950's protest over the use of the subliminals had not been so widespread, the technique would have received thorough testing, allowing advertisers to arrive at a "cost versus return-in-sales" ratio. Subliminals would then have become a potent part of the communications arsenal.[13]

Research did continue quietly, however, and several attempts were made to mechanically manipulate people's minds. *Advertising* magazine re-

---

[12]Key, op. cit. p. 140.
[13]Packard, op. cit. p. 137.

ported rather matter-of-factly that Toyota Motor Sales, USA, was using subliminal images to enhance its commercials.[14]

It was also reported that the British government confiscated a substance discovered by an English chemist to greatly enhance the power of odors to affect the mind.[15]

Furthermore, by 1973, 13 major commercial research firms in the New York, Chicago and Toronto areas were offering a mechanically-induced subliminal message service to advertisers.[16] Even the FCC got into the act! It gave permission for a subliminal message, "Give yourself up," to be flashed on the screen while a midwest television station aired an announcement aimed at a murder-at-large. Skeptics of the effectiveness of subliminals quickly point out the criminal didn't turn himself in, although, whether he ever saw the broadcast is, of course, unknown.[17]

In 1973, however, an advertiser went too far, invading the minds of the younger set. During the Christmas season of that year, a toy manufacturer inserted the words "Get it," flashed four times, at 1/60th of a second in a television commercial for a game called "Husker Du."[18]

---

[14]Ibid.

[15]Lowell Ponte, "Secret Scents That Affect Behavior," *Reader's Digest* magazine (June 1982), p. 122.

[16]Packard, op. cit. p. 124.

[17]Art Athens, "Beward Here Come the Mind Manipulators," *Family Health* magazine (December 1978), p. 39.

[18]Ibid.

When the station technician accidentally spotted the buried commands and reported them to the authorities, the FCC suddenly decided things were getting out of hand. It took the occasion to clarify its position and warned its stations that the use of such techniques was "inconsistent with the obligations of the licensee . . . [and] contrary to the public interest." Though the commercial's subliminals were discarded before the effect could be measured, the FCC said, "Whether effective or not, such broadcasts are clearly intended to be deceptive."[19] Even with the beefed-up regulations, it must be noted, however, that the FCC's focus is only on products sold, not ideas surreptitiously peddled.

In 1974, a Canadian broadcaster uncovered the use of subliminals once again—this time on both the Voice of America and Radio Moscow. It seems we don't want someone to play mind games with our kids, but it's acceptable to do it to someone else's children—in the name of freedom, of course.

Nevertheless, the United Nations launched a study which concluded "the cultural implications of subliminal indoctrination is a major threat to human rights throughout the world," and further, that the modification or even elimination of a culture is possible through subliminal stimula.[20] The United Nations, it appears, was not

---

[19]Ibid.
[20]Key, op. cit. p. 175.

happy with Big Brother's progression from popcorn to propaganda, and quickly condemned the
use of subliminals on international airwaves.

Consequently, hidden messages are supposedly no longer a threat in radio and television
advertising or propaganda. However, that same
sly seduction is still possible in stores, movie thea-
ters, salesrooms, and (yes!) on musical recordings, and it is being used.

One of the greatest difficulties in researching
backmasking techniques, however, is that no
one—whether in the motion picture or the rock
music industry—is willing to admit to using them.
In an informal poll taken of several recording
studios in the Minneapolis/St. Paul area, the recording engineers interviewed confirmed the
feasibility of inserting substimuli into multiple
recording tracks, yet no one would either con-
firm or deny subliminal use in his own studio.

Why not? Two answers seem most obvious:
Either subliminals are *not* being used, but the
public's belief in them jacks up record sales, or
backmasking *is* being used, but those involved
are sworn to secrecy in an effort to avoid civil
liberties lawsuits.

Though this threat of court trials and publicity forces the recording industry to be less than
honest, the retail field has had a heydey with
subliminal techniques.

Becker's Mysterious Little Black Box

The aforementioned Dr. Becker was a prime instigator when he introduced to the retail trade an updated version of the tachistoscope—a contraption he mysteriously christened a "little black box."

Actually, the device is an endless loop cassette player which is capable of receiving, mixing and broadcasting material from two separate sources. Furthermore, it adjusts one of those sources so it is perceivable only subliminally.

The box has been used since 1978, to scramble messages of honesty-inducement with Muzak-like melodies. Blended into the background music of at least 37 stores thus far in the United States (they claim eventually 80 to 90 percent of the retail stores of this country will utilize such a device to stop shoplifting—or for other purposes!)[21] are Becker's little reminders: "Be honest—do not steal. I am honest—I will not steal." The words vary slightly, but the message remains the same, 9,000 times each hour.[22]

Time magazine, who highlighted the device in a 1979 article, describes how it works:

> A shopper in a department store picks up a scarf, glances furtively about, crumples it up and shoves it into her pocket. Then come sec-

---

[21]Ibid., p. 98.
[22]"Secret Voices," *Time* magazine (September 10, 1979), p. 71.

Dr. Becker's "Black Box"
introduces a Dynamic New Era of

BEC's MK VI DIGITAL AUDIO
SUBLIMINAL PROCESSOR
U.S. PATENT 3,278,676

SUBLIMINAL SOUND
from **Behavioral Engineering Corporation**
Specialists in Applied Subliminal Communication [ASC(TM)]

HAL C. BECKER, Ph.D.
President and Director of Research

A Message From Dr. Becker:

"APPLIED SUBLIMINAL COMMUNICATION, ASC(TM), works three principal ways for *loss prevention* and *human resource potentiation:* 1) It enlivens and activates basic wishes and drives, already present in one's unconscious, 2) it imparts new and useful information to one's unconscious, and 3) it increases unconscious selective attention while potentiating awareness.

"Subliminal pyschodynamic activation directly reaches primitive and unconscious levels of the mind and therefore is also useful in a broad range of psychotherapeutic applications, limited only by the ingenuity of the Therapist.

"The BEC Mark VI Digital Audio Subliminal Processor* contains a microprocessor computer with digital speech synthesis circuits to generate subliminal words and phrases for our ASC(TM) techniques. The Processor is entirely solid state. It interfaces readily with any background music system."

Current Applications of ASC(TM)

■ *LOSS PREVENTION*

 Crime Before It Happens —
in Banks, Department Stores, Shops,
Supermarkets, Auto Dealerships

▲ *HUMAN RESOURCE POTENTIATION*

For All People Organizations —
All of the above plus Real Estate Agencies,
Apartment Rental Services, and many others.

IMPROVE: Self-Image, Stress Management, Attitude,
Motivation, and Teamwork to enhance Best Effort

KATHLEEN D. CHARBONNET
Systems Associate
with the BEC MK VI Digital
Audio Subliminal Processor

*Becker, H.C. et al. "Applications of Subliminal Video and Audio Stimuli in Therapeutic Educational, Industrial, and Commercial Settings," Proceedings of Eighth Annual Northeast Bioengineering Conference, Massachusetts Institute of Technology, Cambridge, Mass., March 28, 1980.

Advertisement for Dr. Becker's "little black box."

ond thoughts. She fishes out the scarf, smooths it again, and returns it to the counter. Another victory for honesty? Not quite. Credit for the would-be shoplifter's change of heart really belongs to what the store managers call their "little black box," a kind of electronic conscience. The box is being used to blend the store's background music with the message, "I am honest, I will not steal," repeated rapidly . . . at a very low volume.[23]

Do the devices actually work? One East Coast department store chain paid Becker and his partner, Louis Romberg, a Canadian behavioral scientist, a $10,000 fee for their services. A steep fee, and yet the company reported a 37 percent drop in thefts over a 9-month period. The total amount the company saved was nearly $600,000![24]

This same device—utilizing both audio and video tapes—was recognized by the New Orleans Medical Society as a successful aid for a weight reduction program Becker and Romberg have operated for years. The 12-week program, utilizing subliminally enhanced tapes, has been successful with many office patients, most of whom were physician-referred.

Becker's invention is likewise used by a Toronto real estate agency to inspire its sales personnel with messages such as, "I love real estate.

---

[23] Ibid.
[24] Art Athens, "Beware Here Come the Mind Manipulators," *Family Health* magazine (December 1978), p. 39.

I will prospect for new listings and clients each and every day."[25] Even professional football has gotten into the mind-bending game, utilizing Becker's silent coaching to augment at least one undisclosed National Football League team's pep talks. And hockey's Montreal Canadians use subliminal coaching in the locker room as well.

Eventually, the box's inventor says, he envisions the secreted reminders to take on fairy godmother qualities: "I see no reason why there won't be audio conditioning the same way we now have air conditioning." In fact, he thinks putting subliminals on television, with or without public knowledge, would be a good idea. Of course, he cautions, he would have them directed against such negative situations as drunk driving and drug abuse. "We could eliminate weight problems in our generation, reduce auto insurance by 50 per cent," Becker claims.[26]

What About Abuses?

Becker says he isn't worried about abuses because his little black boxes contain fail-safe mechanisms which bar changes of the subliminal messages within by anyone other than himself. (Of course, this train of thought takes it for granted

---

[25]"Secret Voices," *Time* magazine (September 10, 1979), p. 71.
[26]Ibid.

Becker knows what is best for each one of his unaware listeners.)

Becker says he had originally hoped the users of his device would publicly disclose its presence by posting signs which, for example, in the case of a department store, might state: "You are being treated by our honesty reinforcement and theft deterrent system." So far, however, his customers have refused, fearing negative publicity and action by the American Civil Liberties Union.

Abuses seem even more feasible, given the difficulty of detecting the presence of subliminals. Several researchers have been allowed to review sample tapes, and yet even with sophisticated equipment, have been unable to isolate the subliminals imbedded within.

Furthermore, as pointed out by Wilson Brian Key, in his book *Clam Plate Orgy*, most psychologists are unfamiliar with any of Becker's patented devices, even though dozens of ad executives have been following his subliminal research for years.[27] Consequently, Key pointed out, there is no way to be certain such devices have not been in use for almost 25 years, a fact even more likely, given the American advertising industry's basic moral standard of the "Almighty Dollar."

In late 1983, a small Michigan firm, Stimu-

---

[27] Art Athens, "Beware Here Come the Mind Manipulators," *Family Health* magazine (December 1978), p. 40 & Wilson Bryan Key, *Clam Plate Orgy* (New Jersey: Prentice-Hall, Inc., 1980), pp. 98, 99.

tech, brought the mind-bending business into the computer age. Its home computer kit, Expando-Vision, consists of eight cartridges and a television-to-computer interface. Depending on the program of his choice, a person can now flash goal-oriented messages across his own television screen at the rate of 1/30th of a second every 2½ minutes. The messages, sort of an electronic string-around-the-finger, remind people they are lovable, or successful, or confident. The tapes are designed to help them lose weight, quit smoking, control stress, increase productivity and succeed in a number of other tasks.[28]

This personal use of subliminals seems acceptable. After all, the subject is both aware and receptive to the message. But other uses of subliminals have surfaced lately that are not so healthy.

The Devil Made Me Do It

The film *The Exorcist* is one of three films known to have contained substimuli. Images of blood, ghosts, and death masks are used to enhance the over-all sense of horror the film creates. Warner Brothers, producer of the movie, was sued in 1979 by an Indiana teenager who fainted during the film and broke his jaw. His

---

[28]Felicia Lee, "Whispering Messages to the Mind," *USA Today* (November 4, 1983), pp. 1D, 2D.

lawyer proposed that the fleeting death mask was "one of the major issues of the case."[29]

Another movie, *Texas Chainsaw Massacres*, was selected as the most outstanding film of the year by the London Film Festival in the year it was released, and continues to be a drive-in theater standard feature. Its producer, Tobe Hooper, not only admits subliminals were used to enhance the mood of the movie, but also that "subliminal perception is a killer. The capacity of the unconscious to take information and run with it is unlimited. We flatter ourselves by thinking we are in control of our thinking."[30]

We are also fooling ourselves if we think that subliminals are used by only the television, movie or retail industries. Backmasking, for whatever reason, has occurred on a variety of record albums since the Beatles pioneered the practice in the late sixties. But first, let's try to understand why subliminals can be effective.

[29]"Secret Voices," *Time* magazine (September 10, 1979), p. 71.
[30]*New Times* magazine (May 13, 1977), p. 62.

2

Who Was That Backmasked Man?

A Technical Overview

Coming to Terms

The "subliminal" is the subconscious or deepest part of the mind. Though scientists know the subconscious mind exists, and can measure many of its functions, there is no simple dividing line between it and the conscious mind (the threshold between the two shifts constantly). Then, too, each person is different and even the same individual has different perceptions at different times. Consequently, studies of the complex human mind's functions are difficult and findings are often hotly debated.

One of the contested issues deals with subliminal stimulation, which can come in many forms—words or pictures flashed so quickly we don't consciously remember them, words "masked" by electronic tricks so we don't consciously hear them, or pictures or symbols placed within a work so we don't consciously recall having seen them.

Audio masking makes a sound harder to detect—either by putting noise in front of (forward masking) or behind the sound (backmasking). The term "backmasking" as it is used in this work, however, refers instead to the process of placing secret messages on a recording by any means, whether under, over, backward, forward—or upside down!

No matter by what particular name they are called, all subliminals are, as stated by Dr. Wilson Bryan Key, a prominent researcher in the field, who holds a Ph.D. in communications from the University of Denver and has served as a professor at four prestigious universities, "purposefully designed . . . with the motive of soliciting, manipulating, modifying or managing human behavior."[1]

In other words, the subliminal approach is to serve up a message on which our subconscious brain can feast while our conscious mind goes unaware. The concept of a computer and its programmer provides a fair analogy of the way the brain perceives these secret messages. Our conscious mind is like a computer programmer, who can make value judgments, picking and choos-

---

[1] Wilson Bryan Key, *Media Sexploitation* (New York: Signet Books, 1977), p. 7.

ing the data he wishes, and determining right from wrong.

The subconscious mind, however, is similar to a computer, for the computer doesn't have the power to reason. As the saying goes, "garbage in—garbage out." In other words, it is simply a storehouse for information, whether correct or incorrect.

In the same way, our subconscious mind is also a data base, and its functions don't include the establishing of values.

Some Scientific Jargon

William Yarroll, a neuro-scientific researcher with the Applied Potential Institute in Aurora, Colorado, was a key witness before the California State Assembly's Consumer Protection and Toxic Materials Committee when it met in Sacramento in April 1982. Yarroll studies how the thought processes of the brain function. He says at the base of the brain is a "reticular activating system"—or in laymanese, an editing device. This area contains what is termed the Conditioned Response Mechanism.[2]

This system acts as a programmer to the brain, screening out unwanted or unacceptable information. However, when bits of information are

---

[2]Jacob Aranza, *Backward Masking—Unmasked* (Shreveport, LA: Huntington House, 1983), p. 2.

presented to the mind in covert form, such as by a masking technique, they circumvent this screening procedure, come into the memory unchecked, and are then "decoded" and stored for future use.

According to Lloyd H. Silverman, Ph.D., adjunct professor of psychology at New York University, there are two brain centers that deal with outside stimuli:

> One center is responsible for registering a stimulus, and the other for bringing it into consciousness. The first center is far more sensitive than the second, so that a very weak stimulus [such as low volume words hidden below the music, or inserted backward] will register in the mind, but won't come into consciousness.[3]

The mind doesn't need the information for the moment, so it is placed in a holding pattern before it reaches the conscious level—before the receiver (you) is aware of it.[4] In this way, a notion which most people would reject—such as the statement, "Satan is god"—is allowed to be stored for future access without the usual "once over" inspection.

For example, if a listener received a substimuli that told him stealing was acceptable behavior and would make him happy, and then within a

---

[3]Art Athens, "Beware Here Come the Mind Manipulators," *Family Health* magazine (December 1978), p. 40.
[4]Ibid.

short time, he was in a situation where shoplifting was a real temptation, his subconscious might recall the stored information and use it to determine his behavior.

Silverman's work suggests those people with a strong moral base, such as the Ten Commandments, would not be as susceptible to negative substimuli, however. (Perhaps this should make secular humanists more concerned about being controlled through subliminal commands, since their "If it feels good, do it" behavior can be so easily modified by a hidden message telling them just what does feel good!)

Silverman also demonstrated in his research that subliminally-perceived information can be directly linked to psychopathological behavior. In general, he discovered it is possible to make some individuals either sick or well by exposing them to subliminal messages telling them so.[5]

Another researcher, Wallace LaBenne, a psychology professor and psychotherapist from East Lansing, Michigan, says there are at least 1,000 studies verifying the effectiveness of subliminal messages:

> What we know today is that the brain sees and hears more than the eyes and ears. What we further know is it takes certain frequencies of light and sound for the conscious (mind) to pick it up. We want to bypass the censorship of the left brain (the evaluative and rational

---

[5]Ibid.

side) and go to the right brain (which controls attitudes and habits).[6]

We've seen what subliminal techniques are and what they can do. Now let's take a closer look at the history of subliminals as they appear (or more precisely don't appear) on rock and roll recordings. Interestingly, rock and roll and subliminals were born in the same era.

---

[6]Felecia Lee, "Whispering Messages to the Mind," *USA Today* (November 4, 1983), p. 2D.

3

Rock and Roll Goes Underground

Big Brother Meets the Beatles

In the recording industry, the Beatles were known as innovators: they were the first to employ sophisticated multiple tracks; introduce psychedelics into the music; produce a "concept album"; and elevate album covers to an art form. They were also the first rock group proven to have laid reverse vocal tracks onto a record album.

On their 1968 double album release, *The Beatles*, commonly known as "The White Album," the Beatles hyped a "Paul is dead" sales gimmick with a backmasked message. In the song, "Revolution Number Nine," over and over again at the end of the recording are the lyrics, "number nine, number nine. . . ." If that portion is played in reverse, it was discovered, another set of lyrics comes through: "Turn me on, dead man," ac-

The Beatles as they appeared on the jacket of *The White Album*.

companied by piano playing. Another portion of the same record, played backward, reveals crowd noise and then someone screaming, "Get me out!"

The gimmick worked far better than ever imagined, and soon fans were scrambling for the record, just to ruin their turntables' cartridges and drive systems playing it backward.

Mumble Jumble?

Of course, the Beatles claimed no knowledge of the secret missive, saying any backward message was purely coincidental, and a number of people argue that most of the subliminals documented on records are accidental or that we hear that for which we are told to listen. *Cornerstone* magazine quotes Dr. Israel Goldiamond, a psychology professor at the University of Chicago:

36

Words are not spoken one at a time—you speak in bursts of several words between breaths, with valleys and hills in the sound energy levels coming out of your mouth. The meaning of sound is what we put into it—intelligibility comes out of the code a listener applies. It is only "English" because we have all agreed that certain combinations of sounds and rhythms mean certain things. The effort it would take to say something in English which would mean one thing forwards and another backwards is incredible!

The magazine concludes, "If you are told a mumbling noise sounds like a specific phrase and you listen to it often enough, you may eventually agree the phrase is on the record (when in reality it is a meaningless mumble)."[1]

Though certainly a large number of cases can be chalked up to this phenomenon, Becker himself says the subliminal messages of his black box—messages he personally imbedded—can be heard in the same way: ". . . if you know in advance what phrases to listen for, and if you play the tape in a quiet atmosphere where total concentration is possible."[2] In other words, even when the presence of a subliminal message is confirmed by the scientist who placed it, it often takes prior knowledge of the content of the mes-

---

[1]Ross Pavlac, "Backward Masking: Satanic Plot or Red herring," *Cornerstone* magazine (Volume 11: Issue 62), p. 40.
[2]Art Athens, "Beware Here Come the Mind Manipulators," *Family Health* magazine (December 1978), p. 40.

sage in order for an aware listener to perceive the actual words.

Hidden messages on many groups' albums have been confirmed since the Beatles' "dead man" episode, some employing the backward trick, others recorded at too low a volume to be consciously heard, or recorded forward, but at very high speed. Many messages are obviously inserted intentionally, while still others remain a mystery.

In his book, *Media Sexploitation*, Key mentions that Blue Swede's "Hooked on a Feeling," a 1974 remake of the original B. J. Thomas hit, was the first rock record found to have obscenities embedded in the background.[3] The tune, which was the only real moneymaker for the Swedish rock group, featured a seeming "tribal chant" in the background, which *Who's Who in Rock* describes as "oddly captivating."[4] That background phrase, which sounded something like "ooga-chock-a, ooga-chock-a" to the indiscriminate listener, was responsible for the dismissal of five disc jockeys who, according to Key, played the record on the air, then pointed out what obscenities were being spoken in the background.[5]

Once again, however, it was the Beatles who had perfected the "art." As early as the mid-six-

[3]Wilson Bryan Key, *Media Sexploitation* (New York: Signet, 1977), p. 117.
[4]Michael Bane, *Who's Who in Rock* (New York: Facts on File, Inc., 1981), p. 23.
[5]Key, op. cit. p. 117.

ties, reports *The Rock Book of Lists*, vulgarities, racial slurs and seemingly nonsensical phrases had been implanted on a number of the Liverpool exports' recordings, including "Girl," recorded in 1965; "Baby, You're A Rich Man," recorded in 1967; "I Am A Walrus," also 1967; as well as a number of others.

Electric Light Orchestra entered the subliminals game in 1974 when they produced *Eldorado*, the recording *The Rock Who's Who* says firmly established the group as stars.[6] The album, which eventually was certified gold, is embedded with several backward messages, including, "Christ, you're the nasty one, you're infernal" (meaning hellish, hateful, or abominable), and "He's there on the cross and dead" (inferring Jesus is dead and there is, consequently, no resurrection).

The same group had another hit recording

Album cover for *Face the Music* by Electric Light Orchestra.

---

[6]Brock Helander, *The Rock Who's Who* (New York: Schirmer Books, 1982).

the following year with *Face the Music*, a confusing title, since the main message of the music is
recorded backward. On the cut, "Fire Is High,"
before the lyrics begin, a "secret message" is recorded which, played backward, clearly says,
"The music is reversible, but time is not. Turn
back . . . turn back . . . turn back. . . ."

Bah, Bah Black Sheep

Pink Floyd, that cheery underground group
of loneliness-and-depression fame, had their first
certified platinum award album with *Animals*, released in 1977. On the song "Sheep," from that
LP, there is a distorted rendition of the Twenty-
third Psalm embedded forward on the sound
track. The mocking prayer goes:

> The lord is my shepherd, I shall not want.
> He maketh me to lie down through pastures
> green. He leadeth me the silent waters by; with
> bright knives he releaseth my soul. He makes
> me to hang on hooks in high places. He con-
> verteth me to lamb cutlets. For lo, he hath great
> power and great hunger. When cometh the
> day we lowly ones through quiet reflection and
> great dedication, master the art of karate, we
> shall raise up and then we shall make the bug-
> ger's eyes water. ("Bugger" is a slang term for
> a sodomite—a homosexual or a contemptible
> person with whom sodomy is committed.)

In an even more obvious attempt to sell records—and admittedly, a chance to make sport

Album cover for *Animals* by Pink Floyd.

of the whole subliminal subject—Pink Floyd's
next release, *The Wall*, has the following message
backmasked into the song "Goodbye Blue Sky":
"Congratulations! You've just discovered the secret message. Please send your answer to: 'Old
Pink' in care of The Funny Farm, . . . [the ad-
dress]."

Styx, the group from the windy city of Chicago which sports a mythical name and occultic
connections, featured the occult backmasked on
a number of its songs as well. The tune "Snow-
blind," on its *Paradise Theatre* LP, is a happy-go-
lucky tune about cocaine addiction. When the
lyrics speak of the drug's effect on the body, ask-
ing at one point, ". . . how did I ever get into this
mess?" in reverse it says, ". . . move Satan in our
voices." In addition, the group gave its *Kilroy Was
Here* album a label warning it contained a secret

Outside and inside of album cover *The Wall* by Pink Floyd.

message, presumably as another sales gimmick.

Cheap Trick, another Illinois group, lived up to its name with the album *Heaven Tonight* (1978). The tuneful tricksters recorded The Lord's Prayer at 1/8th speed, then overlaid the song "How Are You" so that the listener would con-

Album cover for
Kilroy Was Here by
Styx.

sciously hear only a faint, chipmunk-like chirp
in the background.

Why The Lord's Prayer? A possible answer
is found in Mike Warnke's book, *The Satan Seller*.
Warnke says that often in occult worship, the
participants chant The Lord's Prayer, either forward or backward, as subtle mockery of God.[7]

A "lord" is mentioned on one of Prince's best-
selling tunes, too, and many have been puzzled
by the apparent Christian element of the backward message. It appears in the song "Darling
Nikki" on the *Purple Rain* LP. At the beginning
of the tune, Prince asks the subliminal question,
"How are you?" Then he lets his fans know, "I
am fine because the lord is coming soon."

When the secret message was discovered,

---

[7]Mike Warnke, *The Satan Seller* (Plainfield, New Jersey: Bridge
Publishing, Inc.).

many teens exclaimed to their puzzled parents, "See, Prince is a Christian! It's okay to listen to his music!" Actually, just the opposite is true.

First, it's important to note the context of the message. Just after Prince's subliminal quote, he launches into a song about his "darling," whom he met (as he describes in lurid detail) after masturbating into a magazine. He cries for his sweetheart Nikki to return so that they can "grind" together as they did in the good old days.

As the Peters brothers have said many times, why look for secret messages in the music when there is so much garbage blatantly displayed up front? There is no socially redeeming value to these lyrics no matter how inviting the melody or talented the musician, or how much is backmasked on the disc.

But what about this reference to a "lord coming soon"? The best answer to that question comes from Scripture. Jesus warned us that not everyone who calls Him "Lord" will enter the kingdom of heaven, but only those who do the Father's will (Matthew 7:21). He also told us at the same time to watch out for "ravenous wolves" who cover up their devious ways with harmless-looking "sheep's clothing." We can discover these false good guys by checking "the fruit" (the result) of their actions.

Though undoubtedly a talented entertainer, Prince's music (the fruit of many hours of labor) is both semi-autobiographical and satiated with sex. One of his first albums, *For You*, was described by *Musician* magazine as having established Prince as "a poetic prince of love, with a mission to spread a sexy message here on earth—a message reinforced by his 'special thanks to God' credit on the LP jacket."

"Prince had heard the call, all right," the magazine explains, "but it wasn't the Lord's sermon that he was preaching, and with his next album, *Dirty Mind*, he catapulted out of the closet and into the public eye as a raunchy prophet of porn" (October 1984, p. 56).

Black Beat magazine tends to agree. They said, "So then, we have to come to the conclusion that the young Prince is well aware of shock value, that his unisexual stage presence, even his narration of The Lord's Prayer during the song 'Controversy,' are all injected to excite or alarm" (April 1983, p. 67). Certainly the message is clear—whether backward or forward—Prince is not led by the Lord, but simply reined by his hormones.

Blue Oyster Cult also used the ⅛th speed technique to record the message, "Furthermore, our father who art in heaven—Satan," on the cut, "You're Not the One," from their *Mirrors* LP, released in 1979.

Satan is also the subliminal subject of a song on the album, *Raunch-n-Roll*, by Black Oak Arkansas. "Black Oak, Arkansas, was once only a place," explains *Who's Who in Rock*, "and that's

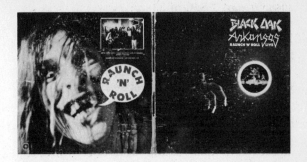

Album cover for *Raunch-n-Roll.*

perhaps what it should have remained. The
group is best known for its sleazy album covers
and raunchy sex lyrics."[8] With that sort of rep-
utation, the backmasking on the song "The Day
When the Electricity Came to Arkansas" seems
right in character. It says, "Satan, Satan, Satan.
He is god, he is god, he is god." Following is what
some listeners say sounds like demonic laughter,
then the chanting of prayers similar to those used
in satanic worship.

Jefferson Starship sings the song, "A Child
Is Coming," on its sci-fi filled 1970 LP, *Blows
Against the Empire*, and tells us everything is getting better with this "child," but the little urchin
is never identified—at least played forward. Play
the tune in reverse, however, and the message is

---

[8]Michael Bane, *Who's Who in Rock* (New York: Facts on File,
Inc., 1981).

46

clear: it says, "Son of Satan."

Anyone—rock fan or not—has probably heard the very popular tune by Queen, "Another One Bites the Dust." It was, for years, often played in ball parks across the country when a player struck out. Played on a echoey, schmaltzy stadium organ, the song perhaps added a touch of humor, but the original recording has imbedded in it a message that isn't funny at all. Repeated four times is the backmasked message, "Decide to smoke marijuana, it's fun to smoke marijuana, decide to smoke marijuana."

The Rolling Stones jumped into the mind-bending business with their *Some Girls* album, released in 1978, which became their best-selling record—over four million copies sold! The title song on that album included a racist, sexist line, "Black girls just wanna get [expletive deleted] all night."

Album cover for Queen's *The Game*, which features "Another One Bites the Dust."

Album cover for *Some Girls* by the Rolling Stones.

Most radio stations across the country refused to play the song because the offensive word is one of seven the U.S. Supreme Court has declared "dirty." New York's "progressive" (their description) rock radio station, WPIX-FM, took another avenue. They simply backmasked the word on the song so that the new version sounded like "humped." The song was still offensive, racist and sexist, of course, but legal. Naturally, other stations quickly got wise to the scam and had a heydey with it, which only served to boost sales further.[9]

Up Jumped the Devil

Following *Some Girls'* success, the Stones wallowed in a mire of bad press and drug problems

_____

[9]*New Times* (August 7, 1978), p. 19.

for some time and enjoyed no outstanding hits. Then in 1980, they returned to the forefront with *Emotional Rescue*, and then *Tattoo You*. Both records went platinum and were followed by a successful tour. The song "Tops," on the *Tattoo* LP, includes as a bogus bonus a backmasked "love song" which says, " 'I love you,' said the devil."

The devil jumps up on a number of albums by the Eagles, Pat Benatar and Led Zeppelin, as well. On the Eagles LP, *Hotel California*, the title cut played forward says, ". . . this could be heaven or hell. . . ." However, when played in reverse the message revealed is: "Yes, Satan, he organized his own religion . . . it was delicious . . . he puts it in a vat and fixes it for his sons and gives it away. . . ."

Pat Benatar, whose lusty love songs have won her three Grammy awards, has several tunes out that seem to have backmasked messages which

Album cover for *Hotel California* by the Eagles.

Grammy-winner
Pat Benatar

promote the devil while dishing the dirt. On the
song "Evil Genius" are the words, "Oh-h, Satan,
that's why I want you to hear my music. The
voice that makes my money."

In "Looking for a Stranger," the singing sex
symbol cries, "I can almost hear you calling, I'm
looking for a stranger in my life." Played in reverse, however, one hears, "And I love it . . . save
us please . . . help us Satan . . . and I love it."

Michael Jackson, the Doobie Brothers, Mot-
ley Crew, AC/DC and Police, Ozzy Osbourne, the
Michael Stanley Band, the Bee Gees and George
Harrison—all have apparent backmasked messages in their music; all mentioning Satan or
making reference to some occultic practice.

Outside and inside of Led Zeppelin's *House of the Holy* album.

But Led Zeppelin—whose most prominent member, Jimmy Page, has demonstrated a great interest in the occult—takes the rock and roll award for ghoulish backward behavior.

In 1975, this band was the most successful group in the world, crowding football stadiums from coast to coast and filling London's 20,000-seat Earl's Court five full days. Howard Mylett, author of two books spotlighting the band, confirms Page's occult leanings and furthermore claims Page has a saying of Aleister Crowley, the infamous satanist, etched into the vinyl of one of the band's records.[10]

It is said the group has hidden a variety of backward communiques on several of its recordings. On *House of the Holy*, the lyrics heard forward are: ". . . is the word that only leaves you guessing. . . ." Played backward, one hears, "Satan is really lord."

The band is at its subtle satanic best, however, with the *Led Zeppelin IV* or *Zoso* LP, a critical and record-breaking success containing the song "Stairway to Heaven," a tune that held the number one spot in popularity for over a decade. Of its hit single, former group vocalist Robert Plant says, " 'Stairway' gets the best reactions of anything we do."[11] Page agrees, saying the song was written in only 15 minutes, shortest of anything they had composed. He added that it felt as if a presence were actually "guiding their pencil across the page."[12]

The song tells of a woman's climb up the stairway to heaven. "There are two paths you can go by," the song tells us, and ". . . you know, sometimes words have two meanings." Played

[10]Yardena Arar, "Coded Messages to the Devil Lurk in Hard Rock?" *The Salt Lake City Tribune* (May 24, 1982), p. A3.
[11]*Circus* magazine (July 1975).
[12]Gary Greenwald, Eagle's Nest Ministries.

Inside cover for Led
Zeppelin's *Zoso* album
which features
"Stairway to Heaven."

backward, the listener can hear the second of
those meanings, but it tells of only *one* path:
"There's no escaping it . . . Here's to my sweet
Satan. No other made a path, for it makes me
sad, whose power is Satan." Another portion of
the record, played forward, says, "There's still
time," but played in reverse yields, "Here's to my
sweet Satan." Elsewhere on the backward side,
according to David A. Noebel, author of a num-

ber of books on rock music, it says, "There was a little child born naked . . . now I am Satan . . ." and "I will sing because I live with Satan."[13]

Play It Again, Sam

The real lies on this recording are in the forward version, however. First, the song says the woman is "buying a stairway to heaven." That's impossible, since heaven can't be earned or bought—it's a free gift. Satan would just love people to fall for that falsehood.

Likewise, the song claims, "There are two paths to go by, but in the long run, there's still time to change the road you're on. . . ." Don't you believe it! The time to choose the narrow path that leads to heaven is today. Don't think you can wait until you're old. Those who live cursing God, most often die cursing Him as well, because their hearts have become calloused— "hardened" as the Bible puts it—and God's invitation can no longer penetrate.

Led Zeppelin's recordings, as many others, prove that even without subliminal stimuli, the lies can be heard loud and clear. The audio masking of secret messages *is* there, however, and in sufficient quantity to make one want to know who is doing it, why are they doing it, does it

---

[13]David A. Noebel, *The Legacy of John Lennon* (Nashville, TN: Thomas Nelson Publishers, 1982).

have persuasive powers, and what should be done about it. In the next chapter, we'll discuss some of the confusing who's and what's of this extremely controversial subject.

4

Big Brother or Big Bother?

Asking the Experts

When considering whether backmasking does exist in today's multi-billion-dollar recording industry, and to what extent, one runs into not a few problems. No one, it seems, wants to talk about it. We are assured by experts, however, that the practice is technically feasible. Says the Salt Lake City Tribune: "Modern multi-track recording equipment allows an artist to record a sound in one direction and then splice it in backward."[1] Likewise, chief engineer for Goodnight Audio, in Dallas, Texas, Tom Gondolf, was quoted: "Quite often on certain pieces of music they will put something in backward."[2]

Commonly accepted examples of backmasking, such as those mentioned on the Beatles', Led

---

[1] Yardena Arar, "Coded Messages to the Devil Lurk in Hard Rock?" *The Salt Lake City Tribune* (May 24, 1982), p. A3.

[2] *The Dallas Morning News* (November 1, 1981), p. 8F.

56

Zeppelin's and Electric Light Orchestra's recordings, serve to authenticate claims of the presence
of backmasking, but as Bruce Helmik, chief recording engineer for Amerisound Studios in Co-
lumbus, Ohio, comments, "Backward masking
does exist, but it's very rare. At studio rates," the
sound tech contends, "it's very expensive because of the technical trouble involved in doing
it well enough so that you can't hear it when
played forward."[3]

And yet, cases do exist. The complexity of
some of these hidden messages seems to defy
human innovation. It seems feasible, therefore,
that the supernatural has sometimes been at work
without the knowledge of the rock musicians or
the recording technicians.

The War Is On

Who, then, do we suspect is doing so much
of this covert communication? One answer can
be found in the Bible. It says the coming Antichrist's trademark is that his mouth will speak
arrogant words and blasphemies, and he will give
his agents power to wage war and blaspheme
against God and His followers (Rev. 13:6, 7).
There is no reason to believe therefore, that Satan can't serve up a secret message on a record

---

[3]Ross Pavlac, "Backward Masking, Satanic Plot or Red Herring," *Cornerstone* magazine (Volume 11: Issue 62), p. 41.

if and when he wishes, since through this technique, he could receive worship from many unknowing fans. This would help explain the many times that words spoken forward say something else entirely when played backward, an audio feat which, as mentioned before, would take a tremendous amount of effort to perform.

Still other instances can probably be chalked up, as previously stated, to the power of suggestion—people do often hear what they expect to hear—or to coincidence or to misinterpretation. Still, however, enough clearly intentional cases have been documented to cause some concern.

Manual on Magic, a Key to Backmasking?

One question we are asked repeatedly is, Why are so many subliminals reportedly recorded backward? One explanation can be found in Aleister Crowley's book, *Manual on Magic*.

Crowley, a notorious mystic, infamous the world over as the most wicked man who ever lived, was known to be a heroin addict, murderer and sexual pervert, and before his death, he actually renamed himself "The Beast 666." In his tome on magic practice, he strongly suggested his followers train themselves to think backward. It was one way, he claimed, they could get insight into the coming world, and he encouraged them to practice writing, listening, speaking, and even walking backward.

Strangely enough, the brain seems able to handle backward images with ease. According to William Yarroll, the creative right hemisphere of the brain does the work. The neuroscientific researcher, who says document forgers have used this principle for years, reveals that making good, hand-written copies of a mirrored image, drawing, letter or signature is not a very difficult task for the brain to handle.[4]

Likewise, Key says "the unconscious system appears able to unscramble even certain kinds of distorted information without individuals becoming consciously aware of the perception . . . a comparable effect can be accomplished with sound-changing speed harmonics in recording. The sound is consciously perceived as jumbled . . . but the information is perceived in its undistorted form at the unconscious level.[5]

In the same way, the study of hypnotism has also shed some light on the brain's ability to pick up backward stimuli. According to Key, "Many people in a hypnotic trance can fluently read upside-down, mirror-image texts, suggesting that the brain can perceive information despite seemingly incomprehensible distortions.[6]

In 1982, the Peters brothers interviewed a famous hypnotist following his appearance on a

[4]*Newsweek* magazine (May 17, 1982), p. 61.
[5]Wilson Bryan Key, *Clam Plate Orgy* (New Jersey: Prentice-Hall, Inc., 1980), p. 87.
[6]Ibid., p. 95.

television talk show in the Cleveland, Ohio, area. He told us he has a cassette tape series available for patients suffering from weight and cigarette-smoking problems. The tapes, he says, consist of music with both forward and backward subliminal messages laid down behind. The hypnotist claimed many persons have been helped by the backmasked aids, adding further credence to the belief that the mind can digest messages in any form.

The notion that there is a relationship between subliminal stimuli and post-hypnotic suggestion is not a new one. Dr. Otto Poetzle was the first to recognize the connection in 1917. He exhibited, according to Key, the power of a subliminal to evoke behavioral response long after the initial introduction of the stimuli was made.

Unfortunately, most of the backmasked messages in rock music are not quite so benevolent as those tried by these two hypnotists! In the music field, the suggestions seem most often to be created specifically to promote satanic hidden agendas. Rock and roll has long been labeled "devil's music" by concerned preachers and parents—often to the great amusement of both rock's stars and fans—and more recently, any search for the truth in the subliminal debate has brought similar "witch hunt" labels upon those involved in the controversy.

Whether these messages are Satan-created, or simply Satan-inspired, subliminal stimuli certainly must have the "Satanic Seal of Approval," for one never hears of secular rock albums promoting secretly the gospel of Christ—or even simply wholesome thoughts, such as "Eat all your vegetables, Maynard," or "Would it hurt to visit your grandmother once in a while?"

Instead, they are always negative, and seem to fit the same six categories of error into which rock music played forward falls: (1) despondency, suicide or escapism; (2) secular humanism and commercialism; (3) rebellion and violence; (4) hedonism (the pursuit of worldly pleasure to the exclusion of spiritual goals); (5) occultism or Satanism; and (6) drug and alcohol use and abuse. (See *Why Knock Rock* for a detailed explanation of these concepts.)

And while the notion of satanic involvement may sound archaic in our modern, technological society, any military strategist will tell you it is dangerous to underestimate the enemy—and foolhardy to pretend he doesn't exist. Satan would love for us to misjudge his powers or activities, or better yet, scorn his existence. After all, he is the master of disguise, and backmasking seems to be a perfect avenue for his trickery. Therefore, although a certain amount of wisdom is needed to forestall a "witch hunt" mentality, it's still perfectly logical to assume satanic involvement in backmasking.

Many other incidences of rock music subliminals are probably the actual work of rock stars,

Mick Jagger, "the
Lucifer of Rock."

their producers or technicians. One reason is, as
Mick Jagger of the Rolling Stones so crassly puts
it, "Satanism sells records."[7] Jagger, who *Newsweek* magazine has described as "the Lucifer of
Rock, the unholy roller," has spoken candidly of
his "power to affect people" (January 4, 1971).

Whether he and others like him use satanic
subliminals as a sales gimmick, a joke, or a deed
done in deadly earnest, these misled unfortu-
nates are flirting with real danger when they
dabble in the occult or black magic—forward or
backward. Playing around with the devil is like

---

[7]Tony Sanchez, *Up and Down With the Rolling Stones* (New
York: William Morrow & Company, 1979), p. 150.

62

playing Russian roulette. Perhaps the first time a person pulls the trigger, the gun won't fire, but if he keeps playing long enough, he's liable to blow his head off. The devil has only one purpose in mind—to see as many souls as possible damned to hell with him. Does that sound like fooling around? Don't be too sure. The Bible says, "It is like sport to a fool to do wrong" (Prov. 10:23, RSV).

!Em Yub—?Sgniht Gniraeh

Another explanation for the profusion of musical subliminals, especially the ones which seem to make no sense, is that they are there simply as a gimmick to sell records. After all, it's time-consuming and expensive, as we have already noted, to perform technical tricks on records, and seasoned businessmen such as the Beatles, Prince and Michael Jackson are not likely to use subliminals just on a lark.

Those seemingly nonsensical words are, in reality, "red flag" words (which verbiage researchers have found provoke an emotional response in people, and are therefore valuable promotional tools).

According to Vance Packard, author of two best-selling books, *The Hidden Persuaders* and *The People Shapers*, certain words are charged with high emotional overtones. Culturally taboo words such as whore, raped, penis, and bitch were given as examples,[8] as well as emotionally-charged words such as death and blood.

In testimony before a New Jersey Assembly Committee, Dr. Robert Corrigan of the Precon Corporation reported that such feelings-generating words can be visually flashed twice to three times as fast as a neutral word such as "river" or "apple" and still cause a later response.

This suggests that the threatening emotion-provoking words were being reacted to and resisted prior to any conscious awareness. Furthermore, research with the motion picture medium supported these results.[9]

Naturally, a person must be at least slightly motivated for the impact to be felt, but many words are tremendously powerful. When used subliminally, either by audio or visual masking, those same words can have a masterful effect on the listener.

Advertising people are now beginning to apply this same technique to television commercials. Electronic specialists, together with psychologists, have created a computerized, voice-compression device that speeds up commercials by as much as 40 percent, without distortion or comprehension loss. The new, jack-rabbit-style commercials are remembered, studies show, far

---

[8]Vance Packard, *The People Shapers* (Boston: Little, Brown & Company, 1977), p. 137.
[9]Key, *Clam Plate Orgy* (New Jersey: Prentice-Hall, Inc., 1980).

better than their tortoise-slow counterparts.[10]

Meanwhile, one of the world's largest advertising agencies, says Packard, forecasts that by 1990, many TV messages will be coming at us in three-second blasts, combining words, symbols and other imagery. "The messages will be almost subliminals," Packard predicts.[11]

This perceptual overload, as Packard suggests, is merely another form of subliminal media strategy. By bombarding individual perceptions with sensory stimuli in heavy quantities or with intense volume, a result similar to hypnotic trance is achieved. "Overload, in effect, performs sensory anesthesia at the conscious level, assuring that media content will reach the unconscious without ever surfacing at the conscious level."[12] (This is the same technique music videos use to keep the viewer "glued" to the screen, and as the data indicates, completely open to the messages contained in the music. For more information on this new form of both subliminal and conscious bombardment of the senses, refer to the book, *Why Knock Rock?*)

This sort of evidence makes it easier to understand why many supposedly nonsensical messages appear on rock records—they are simply

---

[10]Vance Packard, "The New (and Still Hidden) Persuaders," *Reader's Digest* (February 1981), p. 122.
[11]Ibid.
[12]Key, *Clam Plate Orgy* (New Jersey: Prentice-Hall, Inc., 1980), p. 87.

quick, power-packed "flag" words used to grab our subconscious attention.

However, just for the sake of argument, let's discard all but the very intelligible, obviously intentional subliminal messages. Though these are admittedly few in number, the question still remains, can they influence us?

The answer is, at present, highly contested, and hard, unbiased evidence proving subliminals' effects on us is difficult to find. Though most testing does show an effect on behavior and opinions, the jury is still out on the extent of that effect, and many scientists contend the influence is negligible. Let's look at some of the opinions from respected people and publications in the field:

Wilson Bryan Key: "Subliminal technology sells records by the tens of millions·each year in North America. No one apparently knows or understands as yet, however, the consequences of this sensory bombardment upon human value systems."[13]

Furthermore, Key says he found through a series of experiments that subliminal stimuli do have the ability to move a person's "anchor points." These points were in relationship to sound, weight, electrical shock and visual size; however, Key concludes, "It isn't improbable that

---

[13]Wilson Bryan Key, *Media Sexploitation* (New York: Signet, 1977), p. 117.

under intensive, repetitive, and long-term subliminal bombardment, entire value systems could
be arranged."[14]

In addition, he cites experimental data that
suggests exposure to substimuli can change an
individual's evaluation or attitude toward vir-
tually any subject, and he feels that over a period
of time, with enough exposure to a particular
subliminal, many individuals would actually
modify their moral attitudes toward activities as
bizarre as sexual orgies or beastiality.[15]

Michael O'Grady: The intriguing possibility
that a subconscious message can influence behavior has encouraged many good studies, including O'Grady's, a particularly helpful one that
showed ". . . stimuli may affect behavior processes to a measurable degree without the subject's awareness."[16]

Family Health: ". . . Dr. Becker's little black
box apparently *is* producing results . . . It does
seem to alter the behavior of *the young and the
impulsive.* [author's italics] . . . It does seem to
change minds."[17]

Science Digest: "Shevrin [Dr. Howard Shev-

---

[14]Ibid., p. 14.
[15]Key, *Clam Plate Orgy* (New Jersey: Prentice-Hall, Inc., 1980),
   pp. 92, 93.
[16]Michael O'Grady, "Effect of Subliminal Pictorial Stimulus
   on Skin Resistance," *Perceptual & Motor Skills* (44:1051–56,
   1974).
[17]Art Athens, "Beware Here Come the Mind Manipulators,"
   Family Health magazine (December 1978), p. 39.

rin, psychologist at the University of Michigan, and active in subliminal technique research] . . . has been probing electronic responses to subliminal stimulation and has discovered brain-wave 'correlates' that show the brain responding 'differentially' to subliminal messages." In other words, he has discovered electronic impulses registering unique responses to messages received unconsciously.[18]

Shevrin admits we may soon be confronted with the problem of guaranteeing the individual's right to privacy, "the use of brain waves to reveal information customarily protected by the utmost privacy of one's inner thoughts," and expresses concern that techniques such as subliminal suggestion and brain wave research could "in the wrong hands be used for invasive and manipulative purposes" ("Subliminal Perception and Subliminal Communication Technology," report prepared for invited testimony before U.S. Congressional Subcommittee, August 6, 1984).

Dr. Howard Shevrin (psychologist at University of Michigan Hospital): During testimony before the Subcommittee on Transportation, Aviation and Materials of the Committee on Science and Technology of the U.S. House of Representatives, Shevrin also revealed, "Although I do not believe that these subliminal messages

---

[18]R.C. Morse and David Stoller, "The Hidden Message That Breaks Habits," *Science Digest* (September 1982), p. 28.

work at all, if they do work as its advocates believe, then they would be powerful enough to change other behaviors in unexpected ways. On both scientific and moral grounds, I believe that Congress ought to look carefully into the possible dangerous effects on the public of subliminal messages employed to change behavior without the individual's consent. . . . Although this may sound like science fiction, we may be on the threshold of invading the individual's last stronghold of personal privacy—his own inner thoughts."

Lowell Ponte (scientific researcher and writer): The human mind's complexity becomes more apparent almost daily. While some still refuse to admit any link between subliminal suggestion and behavior modification, research continues to point out differently.

According to Ponte, a 1982 study of subliminal odor proved that people can recognize up to 10,000 distinct odors and that the olfactory cells of the nose are directly connected to "rhinencephalon" part of the brain which regulates motor activities such as sex, hunger and thirst.

A biologist, Dr. Robert Henlin of Georgetown University Medical Center, Ponte reports, has found that the U.S.S.R. is using subliminal odors to reduce stress in workers. Dr. Henlin believes certain odors could be used to increase efficiency, reduce aggression, and, if applied to the paper of school textbooks, could encourage students to learn, as well as improve their memory skills![19] In other words, "If it smells good, do it."

While this study isn't quite in line with our research into the secret effects of rock music subliminals, it does graphically demonstrate the power of the subconscious mind to alter our behavior, as well as the power of the subliminal to alter our subconscious mind!

Psychology Today: The magazine relates that Dr. Silverman (mentioned later) believes subliminals affect emotions and can change a person's behavior. He uses a technique called "subliminal psychodynamic activation" to help people read better, lose weight or quit smoking. His series of studies, spanning 10 years, has proven remarkably successful.[20]

Art Linkletter (following the drug-related death of his daughter in 1969): Author Michael Haynes says Linkletter blamed "secret messages" in rock music for "encouraging young people to take part in the growing problem of drug abuse."[21]

Scientist **N. F. Dixon**: In his findings on "The Effect of Subliminal Stimulation Upon Auto-

---

[19]Lowell Ponte, "Secret Scents That Affect Behavior," *Reader's Digest* (June 1982), pp. 122–125.
[20]"Return of the Hidden Persuaders," *Psychology Today* magazine (May 1982).
[21]Michael Haynes, *The God of Rock* (Lindale, TX: Priority Publications, 1982), p. 64.

nomic and Verbal Behavior," Dixon reports: ". . . subliminal stimulus activates primary thought processes.[22] However, in his book, *Subliminal Perception*, he explains some of the difficulties in testing the effects of substimuli: ". . . people evidently prefer to appear insensitive [to subliminals], rather than hallucinated."[23]

Ira Appleman (assistant professor of psychology, Loyola University): "The effects of subliminal manipulation are small and controversial. It's hard to study. How do you know whether something was subliminal or not? Subjects may be unwilling to tell you."[24]

Lloyd Silverman: In his research report entitled "A Clinical Application of Subliminal Psychodynamic Activation," the scientist concludes: "Subliminal symbiotic stimulation, together with self-focusing, offers promise for enhancing the therapeutic value of hospitalization for schizophrenics."[25]

Newsweek (quoting California state Assemblyman, Phillip D. Wyman): " 'Some people believe that the messages [backmasking on rock re-

---

[22]N.F. Dixon, "The Effect of Subliminal Stimulation Upon Autonomic and Verbal Behavior," *The Journal of Abnormal and Social Psychology* (Volume 57: 1958).

[23]N.F. Dixon, *Subliminal Perception* (London: McGraw-Hill, 1971).

[24]Pavlac, op. cit. p. 41.

[25]Lloyd Silverman, "A Clinical Application of Subliminal Psychodynamic Activation," *Journal of Nervous and Mental Disease* (Volume 161: Issue 6).

cords] can manipulate our behavior without our knowledge or consent and turn us into disciples of the antichrist.' Last month the California Assembly's consumer-protection committee listened to a selection of 'backwardly masked' records. . . . The committee, somewhat skeptically, recommended full-scale hearings this fall on a bill that would require warning labels on all records carrying subliminal messages."[26]

St. Paul Dispatch: "As a result of findings that rock records contain subliminal messages, California Assemblyman Phillip Wyman has proposed a state law requiring records containing subliminal messages to bear a warning label. Wyman answers his critics, who contend he is attempting to legislate morals, 'I don't care, as a legislator, what the message is.' "[27]

George Stephen (researcher): In his treatise entitled "Effect of Subliminal Stimuli on Consumer Behavior: Negative Evidence," Stephen finds that the studies which had positive results indicated that thresholds vary considerably from individual to individual and are affected by many uncontrollable factors, making it extremely difficult to provide stimuli which are both unnotice-

---

[26] "American Graffiti," *Newsweek* magazine (May 17, 1982), p. 61.
[27] *St. Paul Dispatch* (May 24, 1982).

able and yet effective with a large group of people.[28]

Newservice: "Following an unprecedented series of studies at Canada's University of Lethbridge and reported in *Science 83*, psychologists John Vokey and Donald Read argue that backward-masked messages have no demonstrated effect on human behavior. . . . So backward-masked messages can indeed be found in music or tapes, although whether or not they're built-in intentionally to seduce young minds or confound older ones is still a matter of debate.

"According to Vokey and Read's studies, the messages exert little, if any, influence on behavior and are of dubious value. . . . Even more pointless, Vokey and Read conclude, are legislative measures to protect the public from their own imaginations."[29]

An amusing, yet thought-provoking, commentary on the advertising industry's study of subliminals is found in the same magazine. On page two of *Newservice*, we see an ad proclaiming in quarter-inch-high type: "SUBLIMINAL PERSUASION: The Effortless way to change your life. . . . Now from Potentials Unlimited comes a series of subliminal tapes with sugges-

[28]George Stephen, "Effect of Subliminal Stimuli on Consumer Behavior: Negative Evidence," *Perceptual & Motor Skills* (Volume 41: 1975), pp. 847–854.

[29]"Newsfronts—Behavior: The Devil and Rock 'n' Roll," *Newservice* magazine (November/December 1983), p. 11.

tions to improve your life ... designed so you can use them at any time ... as you work, read, relax, or even sleep ... powerful methods to improve your mind." One has to wonder what ad agencies know that scientists have yet to discover, when the agencies spend thousands of dollars promoting and selling the same subliminals scientists tell us have "no demonstrated effect on human behavior."[30]

Aryeh Neier (former executive director for the ACLU): "People have a right to go about their business without being subjected to manipulation they don't even know about."[31]

Saturday Review (editorial): "The subconscious mind is the most delicate part of the most delicate apparatus in the entire universe. It is not to be smudged, sullied, or twisted in order to boost the sales of popcorn or anything else. Nothing is more difficult in the modern world than to protect the privacy of the human soul."[32]

Confused?

Perhaps now the dilemma is more obvious to see. How do we measure something we can't

[30]*Newservice* magazine (November/December 1983), p. 2.
[31]"Secret Voices," *Time* magazine (September 10, 1979), p. 71.
[32]*Saturday Review* magazine editorial, as cited in "Sneaky Substimuli and How to Avoid Them," *Christianity Today* magazine (January 31, 1975), p. 9.

hear? How do we test subliminal's effects on behavior objectively? After all, we can't follow test
subjects around forever. How do we even legislate violation of privacy when subliminals are so
difficult to isolate (audio subliminals are, in fact,
nearly impossible to isolate) and so impossible to
find agreement on? How do we regulate subliminals when the media, especially the music industry, is unwilling to admit their existence?

In the next chapter, we'll look into the subject
from the Christian point of view and discuss some
criteria helpful for discernment not only on subliminals in rock music, but on rock music in general.

5

Looking for the Obvious
Coming to Our Senses Concerning Subliminals

Obviously, when it comes to the subject of subliminals, the questions on the issue outnumber the answers. So, what's a person to do?

Well, in most cases, a simple look at the album cover or lyric sheet will be enough on which to base a solid judgment. When nudity, occultic practices, mutilation and allusions to drugs are clearly shown in the album art, it's fairly accurate to assume the record's content won't be much more uplifting. Likewise, if the subject matter of the rock album is negative, why look any further?

Another gauge of any particular rock group's music is an examination of any intentions they espouse. Paul Kantner, of the Jefferson Airplane, once boasted, "Our music is intended to broaden the generation gap, to alienate children

The Jefferson
Airplane as
pictured in their
Flight Log album.

from their parents, and to prepare people for
the revolution." One need not look backward into
the music of such a group to discover whether
the content is upbuilding.

Then, too, a review of a rock star's lifestyle
can also be helpful. After all, if a rock celebrity's
life is a mess, he probably has nothing good to
say, forward or backward. But make no mistake:
what he has to say *can* affect you.

Music Hath Charms

You can be certain of this: music affects every
one of us to one degree or another. Ancient history and modern research agree on that much
at least.

The Greek Plato and his philosophizing companions were well aware of the effect of music
on us physically, emotionally and spiritually. In
his work, *The Republic*, Plato contended that mu-

sic could (1) strengthen a person, (2) cause him to lose his mental balance, or (3) cause him to lose his normal willpower so as to render him helpless and unconscious of his acts.[1] The effects—positive or negative—depended, Plato said, on the type of music used.

William Congreve, a 17th-century writer of comedies, agreed with the ancients when he said, "Music hath charms to soothe a savage beast, to soften rocks, or bend a knotted oak."

The Reformers also concurred with the philosopher's assessment. In the preface to the *Wittenburg Gesangbuch* of 1524, Martin Luther provided some insights into music's powerful persuasion when he wrote, "I wish that the young men might have something to rid themselves of their love ditties and wanton songs and might instead of these learn wholesome things and thus yield willingly to the good."

Scientists Confirm Longstanding Beliefs

Though their opinions were expressed hundreds, even thousands, of years ago, according to modern researchers, Plato, Congreve and Luther were all very close to the mark. Scientists today tell us we do indeed respond to music in many measurable ways. Tests have shown music

---

[1]Richard D. Mountford, "Does the Music Make Them Do It?", *Christianity Today* (May 4, 1979), p. 21.

to affect physical changes such as heart rate, blood pressure, respiratory rate, skin sensitivity and muscle control.

Likewise, but in a much more personal way, music has been shown to affect our mood and behavior. Dr. George Stevenson, Medical Director of the National Association for Mental Health, Inc., makes this appraisal: "The widespread occurrence of music among widely distributed peoples and varied cultures is evidence that in music we have a great psychological force."[2]

Rock music, in particular, has been demonstrated to be both powerful and addictive, as well as capable of producing—according to some authorities—a subtle form of hypnosis in which the subject, though not completely under trance, is still in a highly suggestible state.[3]

According to studies by Dr. John Diamond, published in the book *Are the Kids All Right?*, "No parental or police restraint is likely to override a suggestion made through effective hypnosis if it is implanted firmly and often enough on a subject in a receptive sensitized state."[4]

Since the average teenager spends about 6½ hours a day listening to rock music, the possibility of a musical message being "implanted firmly

---

[2]Dr. George Stevenson, *Music and Your Emotions* (New York: Liveright Publishers, Inc., 1952), p. 97.
[3]John G. Fuller, *Are the Kids All Right?* (New York: Times Books, 1981), pp. 239–240.
[4]Ibid., p. 240.

and often enough" is certainly sufficient to cause concern.

This and many other studies suggest rock music's impact on the young listener can be devastating. In fact, according to the Canadian Press Wire Service, the effect of heavy metal rock music so influenced a young Canadian named James Jollimore, that ". . . on New Year's Eve [1983], he went out and stabbed someone, a murder trial has been told." A friend of the defendent testified that Jollimore, 20, who is charged with the first-degree murder of a 44-year-old woman and her two sons, felt like stabbing people when he heard music such as Ozzy Osbourne's *Bark at the Moon*. "Jimmy said that every time he listened to the song he felt strange inside," the friend told the court. "He said when he heard it on New Year's Eve he went out and stabbed someone."[5]

This is not to suggest, of course, that anyone listening to rock music is going to commit mayhem, but to demonstrate its potentially dramatic (and dangerous) influence. Another striking case in point is the impact the Beatles have had on this country. In his research, Key examines song titles created before, during and after their meteoric public career and concludes that the Beatles' main contribution to western society was the way they "popularized and culturally legitimized

[5]"Rock Sparks Stabbing," *Canadian Press Association*: Halifax, Canada (September 26, 1984).

Album cover for
Ozzy Osburne's *Bark
at the Moon*.

hallucinatory drug usage among teenagers
throughout the world.[6]

It seems Plato's fear that "citizens would be
tempted and corrupted by weak and voluptuous
airs and led to indulge in demoralizing emotions"[7]
was well founded. Society's quick acceptance of
previously held taboos coupled with the sudden
rise of rock and roll music as the voice of its
youth indicates there is some cause-and-effect
relationship between the two.

Rock music's promoters have long known the
effect their music can have. The late Jimi Hen-
drix, one of rock music's greatest guitarists, told
Life magazine:

Atmospheres are going to come through

[6]Wilson Bryan Key, *Media Sexploitation* (New York: Signet
Books, 1977), p. 138.
[7]Ibid., p. 118.

music, because music is a spiritual thing of its
own. You can hypnotize people with music,
and when you get people at the weakest point,
you can preach to them into the subconscious
what we want to say.[8]

Of course, we don't fall in a moment, but
according to Dr. D. G. Kehl, of Arizona State
University in Tempe, "Sin has both an accumu-
lative and a domino effect. Satan plants subtle
suggestions, often subliminal ones; he influences
an attitude; makes a 'minor' victory—always in
preparation for the big fall, the iron-bound
habit."[9]

Lotsa Garbage

Consider Lot as an example. He was a righ-
teous man, living with his godly uncle, Abraham.
He knew right from wrong, and further, he desired what was right. However, years spent in
Sodom changed Lot. Though he still desired what
was right, his judgment was affected by the moral
garbage dump in which he lived. When angels
of the Lord came to destroy Sodom, and were
nearly attacked by the men of the city who desired them for homosexual relations, Lot offered instead his own virgin daughters for his
neighbors to gang rape! It wasn't that Lot didn't

---

[8]*Life* magazine (October 3, 1969).
[9]"Sneaky Substimuli and How to Avoid Them," *Christianity
Today* magazine (January 31, 1975), p. 10.

love his daughters, or that he desired them harmed. He simply no longer knew right from wrong. For too long he had been "oppressed by the sensual conduct of unprincipled men" (2 Pet. 2:7, NASB).

Likewise, David was a man after God's own heart, and Samson was a warrior of the Lord, and yet, each of them fell into wrong-doing because they allowed themselves to remain in questionable surroundings where, as Lot, they were open to subliminal persuasion.

The Bible warns us to beware, "lest Satan should get an advantage of us" (2 Cor. 2:11). If you have never made Jesus Christ the center of your life, accepting Him as your Savior, then you need to know you are in a *very* vulnerable position—one in which Satan can certainly take advantage of you. Accepting Christ is a simple yet profound step, however, and you can do so at any time. Don't put off receiving the Lord. He can truly make life worth living. If you wish to know Jesus in a new way, turn to page 104 of this book for help ("Steps to Accepting Jesus Christ").

If you're a born-again Christian, remember we don't fight against simply earthly persuasions, but "against the rulers, against the authorities, against the powers of this dark world and against the spiritual forces of evil in the heavenly realms" (Eph. 6:12, NIV). We need to be aware that Satan will use whatever method he wishes, even rock music, to make us ineffective warriors for Christ, rob us of the joy of a Christian way of life, and even cause us to turn from God.

Does this mean rock music is always bad? Not intrinsically, not by its very nature. Music is a creative force, and all creative forces are God-given and therefore good. But man gets in there and makes rubbish of a lot of God's creation, and Satan, too, has done his share of foul work. As a result, much of the value of secular music has been destroyed.

Writing in the *American Journal of Psychiatry*, Dr. Howard Hansen says music is "made up of many ingredients and, according to the proportions of these components, it can be soothing or invigorating, ennobling or vulgarizing, philosophical or orgiastic. It has powers for evil as well as for good."[10]

That's why we have written books such as *Why Knock Rock?* and *The Peters Brothers Hit Rock's Bottom* to give you, the listener, the proper criteria by which to judge music, and to help you become more aware of the spiritual danger in which you place yourself by listening to hour after hour of questionable rock music.

The fact is, we're much more concerned about

---

[10]Dr. Howard Hansen, *American Journal of Psychiatry*, as quoted by Dr. David A. Noebel, "Christian Rock: A Stretegem of Mephistopheles" (Manitou Springs, CO: Summit Youth Ministries), p. 6.

rock's musical messages recorded and played forward than backward. For whether or not one accepts the belief that backmasking registers in the mind and affects future behavior, one must agree that listening repeatedly to records that openly promote dubious or harmful values does basically the same thing.

(The question-and-answer section following this chapter will highlight some common questions we hear concerning rock music, but if you need more information in order to make educated choices, look for details of other helpful rock music materials available in the "Resources" section: Appendix 3.)

The bottom line of most messages presented by the media today is, as Ernest Dichter, president of the Institute for Motivational Research, Inc., says, ". . . to give moral permission to have fun without guilt."[11] However, we question whether the media has the right to advocate as "fun" various types of perversion and illegal practices—especially the rock music media, whose prime target audience includes eight- to twelve-year-olds.

Rock Music—A Reflection or a Persuader?

When asked about the morality of such practices, Joseph Smith, board chairman of Electra

---

[11]Ernest Dichter, president of Institute for Motivational Research, Inc., as quoted by Vance Packard, *The Hidden Persuaders*, p. 243.

Asylum Records, defended rock producers. On the program *ABC Nightline*, he argued that they didn't intentionally produce records designed to corrupt youth. Instead, he offered, artists have enough trouble to rhyme lines, let alone worry about morality. Besides, Smith contended, hadn't kids already learned about all these practices from television and their peer groups at school? And didn't music artists merely reflect society's values, not promote new ones?

Perhaps some of the values promoted by rock music are considered acceptable by a small segment of society, but to grant the modern-day philosopher, the rock musician, total freedom to preach whatever "gospel" he wishes on our public airwaves without concern is a ludicrous misinterpretation of the First Amendment.

In actuality, there is no "freedom of expression" clause in the First Amendment. However,

One of rock's modern-day philosophers: Prince.

there *is* provision in the Federal Communications Code (Title 18, Section 1464) for those who broadcast perversion to minor children: the clause spells out both fine and jail sentence as appropriate punishment for offenders. There are many more arguments as well for judicial sanctions against overt, as well as subliminal, violations against the public good.

In the next chapter, we'll discuss what the so-called "experts" on this hotly debated issue suggest be done to make subliminals criminal, and we'll interview some of the governmental people working toward a legislative solution.

6

Big Brother Meets Uncle Sam

Current Legislative Attempts to Silence Subliminals

Knowing backmasking is not only feasible as a technical trick, but in all probability, also effective as a persuader, the question must be asked: What is being done to control the use of subliminals? Though the jury is still out on the extensiveness and effectiveness of substimuli, several recent efforts have been made to curb them.

California Assemblyman Phillip Wyman is convinced rock musicians frequently record messages backward on their albums. He is also sure that it can sometimes be harmful to the listener and that something ought to be done about the situation. He has proposed a law in his home state that would require any records containing subliminal messages to be labeled accordingly: "Warning: this record contains backward masking which may be perceptible at a subliminal level when the record is played forward."[1]

Though his critics contend Wyman is attempting to legislate morality, he says, "I don't care, as a legislator, what the message is."[2] Wyman's concern, according to his aide, Jim Meyer, is consumer protection. "Our bill requires disclosure if using subliminal techniques, not a banning of the product. We're approaching the use of subliminals as a consumer's problem. We simply want the consumer to get more protection."

Wyman originally presented his case for the necessity of subliminal regulation to an Assembly Consumer Protection and Toxic Materials Committee meeting convened in the spring of 1982. Results of those hearings were hotly contested and several of Wyman's key witnesses—among them, Yarrow, Silverman, Becker and Shevrin (all mentioned earlier)—were challenged for both their conclusions and credentials.

Says Wyman's aide of the controversy, "There is a tremendous diversity of opinion on this issue, and no real consensus at this point. But I don't think the people called before the committee are trying to con anyone." He did concede, however, that some do make claims they can't back up.

[1]"Satanic Messages Heard in Rock Music," *St. Paul Dispatch* (May 24, 1982).

[2]Yardena Arar, "Coded Messages to the Devil Lurk in Hard Rock?", *The Salt Lake City Tribune* (May 24, 1982), p. A-3.

Subliminals Laws Take a Bad Turn

Though Wyman's law eventually passed the lower house of the California state legislature, it became stalled in committee on the Senate side. Eventually, much of the original data supporting the bill was labeled too dated by members of the Senate committee. Consequently, Wyman's office is now conducting research to discover to what extent subliminals are still being used.

Attempts to legislate against subliminals took a similar bad turn in Arkansas recently. Though the law was eventually passed in that state, it was recently shot down by their courts on the basis of constitutionality. Further attempts at reconstruction of the regulation remain to be seen.

According to Meyer of California, the decision to proceed once again with legislation in his state will depend, to a large degree, on findings by a United States Congressional subcommittee presently investigating the same matter. "It's about a two-year process to bring about a new law," Meyer explains. "It takes a lot of time. Once we hear what has happened on the subcommittee on Science and Technology, and can see their documentation, we can make a decision as to whether to renew our efforts."

Democrat Don Glickman of Kansas is responsible for proposing the national-level hearings. Though a determination to initiate legislation has not been made yet (that will be decided at the next session of Congress), Glickman is bothered by the ethical issues involved with the use of subliminals. "Though the outcome of the hearings is difficult to assess," Glickman's aide, Curt Stanford explains, "a consensus began to develop as the hearings proceeded, that the use of such techniques when the person is unaware is unethical, whether the subliminal works or not."

Stanford says they will most probably proceed with legislation which would call for public notice when subliminals are used, and would be aimed specifically at the expanded home video tape market as well as retail outlets' attempts to curb shoplifting subliminally. Though not expressly geared to subliminals on recordings, the law could easily be applied to such cases as well, *if* they can be substantiated.

Therein lies the problem: getting hard evidence. "One aspect of this topic," says Meyer, "is that many people involved with allegedly developing and marketing subliminal techniques don't want to disclose what they know for three reasons: (1) the fear of regulation; (2) the desire to stay very secretive—after all, the very purpose of subliminal stimulation use is to have a competitive edge over the next guy; (3) the reality that once known about, subliminals are no longer subliminal."

Assemblyman Wyman's aide further suggests that if California were to pass legislation prohibiting subliminals, the bill could be policed only through the state's department of consumer affairs. "They would be in charge of regulating and enforcing the law, relying to a large extent on consumer complaints, and also possibly some independent investigation."

Likewise, Glickman's national law, if proposed, would attempt to protect the public in the same way, by relying on consumer input. Anything beyond that, concede both legislators, would be nearly impossible to enforce, since subliminals are meant to be neither seen nor heard. How then, one might ask, is the consumer supposed to complain if he is unaware of the subliminal's presence?

The Catch-22 of subliminal regulation, then, is that although the FCC has ruled subliminal techniques inconsistent with the public charter granted to the broadcasting industry, and has banned their use across the board, and though the FTC has decreed subliminals not be used for trade purposes, and though state and national legislators have repeatedly called before committees a variety of scientists, psychologists, media experts, government officials, and attorneys who testify to the power and use of subliminals, one cannot police something one can neither see nor hear.

Much Ado About Nothing?

The probable outcome of this revived fuss over subliminals' effects on an unknowing public will no doubt be a return to the pattern cut out in the 1950's: after discovery came public outcry; then pressure for legislation; next, pompous oratory and expensive committee assemblies; and finally, nothing. Even a promise from the offending industries that they would "be good" would be some consolation. However, though W. Howard Chase, president of the Public Relations Society of America, admits, "The very presumptuousness of molding or affecting the human mind through the techniques we use has created a deep sense of uneasiness in our minds,"[3] that "uneasiness" has done little to change their tactics.

It is time for concerned people to push the issue further. Does not our society, born on the ideals of free speech, have the right to control media messages, whether delivered openly or by backmasking techniques? According to Key, there are a variety of arguments for judicial sanctions of subliminal techniques, including common law, nuisance doctrine, trespass, constitutional notions of the right to privacy and due process of law, health considerations and even existing rulings of federal regulatory authority such as the FCC and the FTC.[4]

Though the search for an ethical conclusion

[3]Vance Packard, *The Hidden Persuaders* (Boston: Little, Brown & Co., 1957), p. 243.

[4]Wilson Bryan Key, *Media Sexploitation* (New York: Signet, 1977), p. 190.

is a difficult one, we as Christians have a responsibility to check in every way possible the corruption of our society by whatever means, and that includes subliminal seduction. In his book *Corporate Ethics: The Quest for Moral Authority*, George Forell says, "The social irresponsibility of corporations is . . . the resulting defect of the men and women who have worshipped the golden calf of idolatry. In view of this danger, the religious community should carefully and persistently work in the direction of greater corporate responsibility. . . . The Christian community should try to make available its particular insights and thus become one significant source of authority for the corporation."[5]

In other words, one of the main ways we as Christians can have an effect on our environment is also one of the most obvious—and the most often overlooked. Contribute. Participate. Make a difference in your community. Get involved in local politics. Become a regular correspondent to your representatives in both state and national government. Let them know how you feel about being secretly manipulated by the media.

Of course it takes time and commitment. But too often we Christians hide behind what evangelist Bob Mumford describes as a "back to the

---

[5]George Forell, *Corporation Ethics: The Quest for Moral Authority* (Philadelphia: Fortress Press, 1980), pp. 62–63.

fort" mentality—just hanging on until Jesus comes. Never mind that people are outside the fort, dying for lack of wisdom. On the contrary, Jesus commanded every Christian go out and be a witness "to the ends of the earth" (Acts 1:8, NIV). Does that sound like a life led timidly behind fortress walls? Of course not! If we are to be the salt of the earth, as Jesus urged us, we'll need to jump right into the stewpot.

The 18th-century English statesman and orator, Edmund Burke, once said, "The only thing necessary for the triumph of evil is for good men to do nothing." Whether it's fighting for laws banning subliminals from rock music and advertising, or calling for the rating of morally-degrading rock records, we need to stand up and be counted; furthermore, we need to be willing to inform others.

It is a ludicrous comment on Christians' lack of social involvement that every nuance of racism and bigotry has been removed from public textbooks in the fear that showing Janie washing dishes in a third-grade reader might forever relegate the book's female readers to domestic tasks, and yet we allow to continue an onslaught of both subliminal and conscious blows to the moral fiber of our society through rock music and the media.

In addition to making a "corporate" decision to get involved, we need to make a private decision concerning rock music and the media in general. We need to "take out the garbage" in our own homes before we can criticize our neighbor's trash heap.

As Francis Schaeffer, the Christian philosopher, author and theologian, told *New Wine* magazine in an interview, "After we become Christians, our primary responsibility is to affirm the existence of God by exhibiting His character. . . . As Christians, in everything we do we should exhibit the character of God."[6]

Instead of residing in our "Christian ghettos," Schaeffer urges we face the battle, stand and fight:

> [We must] have the courage to look at the faces of modern culture and to realize why they are empty. We must recognize that modern art and thinking are shaped by the modern secular world view which claims that impersonal matter or energy formed by chance— not a personal God—is the final reality. That secular world view is causing a complete collapse of culture, a tremendous victory for Satan. . . . Each of us must be willing to pay the price of commitment to the living God in our own profession and sphere of responsibility, regardless of what that price may be. When we are willing to pay that price, then we will truly be living on the cutting edge.[7]

---

[6]"An Interview with Francis Schaeffer, The Battle for Our Culture," *New Wine* magazine (February 1982), p. 4.
[7]Ibid., p. 9.

Appendix 1: Questions Most Often Asked About Rock Music

Do you think rock music will send me to hell?

Rest assured, nothing and no one can "send" you to hell—the devil, your friends, movies, nor any kind of music. The only way you can be sent to hell is if you send yourself. You are responsible for yourself and your actions; no one or nothing else can get the credit or the blame.

What other people and things *can* do, though, is provide an occasion to sin; and it is unforgiven sin which can keep you from an eternity spent with the Lord.

As an occasion to sin, rock music can cause both confusion and temptation. It can trip you up, muddy your thinking and misguide your actions. That is where rock's danger lies. If you're smart, and concerned about your eternal welfare, you'll avoid rock music and all its sneaky snares.

Why don't you have documentation on all the latest groups?

Since the music scene changes at an unbelievable rate, a group blasting the charts this week may be gone and forgotten the next. Magazines and newspapers shy away from the latest rages until they look as if they will be established hits for some time to come. Otherwise the publisher's material, which is often written months in advance, might be outdated before it ever hits the racks. Then, too, some groups don't want to grant very many interviews for fear they will suffer from negative publicity before they have carved their own niche in the rock music scene.

Then how can I tell if the group I like plays music I can listen to without danger?

Our list of rock celebrities and bands doesn't have to be all-inclusive. You can judge any rock group yourself by the following criteria:

1. **LIFESTYLES.** 1 Corinthians 15:33 says, "Do not be fooled. 'Bad companions ruin good character'" (GNB). Examine the lives of the rock groups to which you listen. Are their lifestyles promoting and encouraging you to be more Christlike? Do they seem to be peaceful, filled with joy, or are they using "crutches" such as drugs, alcohol, or promiscuous sex in order to maintain a false front of happiness?

Remember, knowing Jesus Christ as your personal Savior is not a religion; it's a relationship, a lifetime experience. If you're going to live the Christian life, you'll need to surround yourself with people who exemplify that lifestyle. Can you say that about your rock star "companions"?

2. **LYRICS.** You need to pay attention to the lyrics of the tunes your favorite rock groups sing. According to *Psychology Today*, when asked whether they were more interested in the sound or in the meaning of the lyrics of songs, 70 percent of the teens polled responded they like a record more for its beat than for its message.

However, whether you are conscious of the message or not, the lyrics *can* still have an effect. In addition, you do pick up the words to songs even when you don't realize it. When we give seminars, we often play snatches of popular tunes, and each time we stop the music, we can hear most of the teens present singing along, even though they claim they don't listen to the words.

Lyrics need to be studied in two ways:

First, what is actually being said? Is it morally unacceptable or degrading to the human spirit? Could it cause feelings of depression or anxiety, or tempt you to use drugs? Does it encourage or discourage your growth as a Christian?

Second, how do the lyrics affect you personally? Not everyone responds to music in the same way—it's a fairly personal encounter. According to Richard D. Mountford, a music professor at Malone College in Canton, Ohio, "Highly personal associations can emerge when we hear music which we encounter at a time of emotional stress or exhilaration. Psychologists call such an association 'classical conditioning' or 'signal learning.' " Mountford continues, "This conditioning is resistant to our efforts to be free of it, and Christians must be conscious of its effect upon them" (*Christianity Today* magazine, May 4, 1979, p. 22).

Check yourself when you're listening to your favorite tune. Even if it is essentially a perky, upbeat song, it can make you feel like singing the blues if you associate it with your long-lost old flame. If the music isn't building you up, it's not for you no matter what it's about.

3. **GOALS.** Make no mistake about it, even apparently only-out-for-a-good-old-time rock groups have definite goals in mind for their music. Some have hidden agendas, while others are quite upfront concerning what they're all about. Check into your favorite group and discover what they hope to accomplish through their music. Magazine interviews can be very telling.

Music was created by God as an expression of the soul and was intended to praise Him and edify others. Does your favorite musician intend to enhance your relationship with Jesus? Don't be in the dark about his goals for you. Scripture says we should always be aware of what the devil's plans are for us "in order to keep Satan from getting the upper hand over us" (2 Cor. 2:11, GNB). To do that, we must be ready to dig a little bit into the backgrounds of rock stars and discover if their intentions coincide with God's or Satan's.

4. **GRAPHICS.** Perhaps you can't judge a book by its cover, but you can tell something about the content of a record by its album cover. Ask yourself, what is the cover portraying: Sex? Pornography? Sensuality? Violence? Occultic practices? Demons? Eastern religions? Sexual deviance? Many album covers graphically display the dark side of rock music, with all its sin and error in full view.

Don't make the mistake of thinking these things cannot affect you, for the Scripture says, "The eye never has enough of seeing, or the ear its fill of hearing" (Eccles. 1:8, RSV). In other words, your eyes can never see enough filth to be satisfied once you begin looking at it; and your ears will never be satiated once you start filling them with garbage. It's a sad but true fact of our fallen natures, but luckily the opposite is also true. We can counteract these corrupting influences by filling our lives with good, nourishing sights and sounds. And when we do, the result is inner growth and a hunger for more good things.

The decision, however, is a personal one. The world provides more than enough ways to tempt your eyes and ears. It takes conscious, personal effort to avoid those potentially harmful influences, but the rewards more than equal the effort.

Why do the Peters brothers pick on rock music alone, when country western, blues and "easy listening" music can sometimes be just as bad?

You're right! Many other styles of music have been just as guilty of being a corrupting influence on their listeners, and we have sometimes discussed their faults. However, we have conducted most of our research in the area of rock music for two reasons. First, our own congregation, Zion Christian Life Center, was the first to hear our rock seminar. They were a young group at the time, with a median age of only 21. Therefore, not many of them were spending their leisure hours listening to Wayne Newton, Muddy Waters or Burt Bacharach. We could see that they were at a highly impressionable age and that they were experiencing the harmful effects of rock music in their personal walks with the Lord.

Second, in the last 15 years, rock artists have become much more militant and more apt to blatantly advocate and promote morally objectionable "alternate lifestyles." Though we aren't saying *all* rock bands advocate harmful or immoral lifestyles, we do contend that enough of them do—and blatantly so—for it to be of major concern to all young people and their parents.

How can I rid my life of the effects of rock music? Where do I start?

It's a decision you'll have to make for yourself. No one else can make it for you. Once you have decided to give up rock music, or a particular group which you feel is harming you, do whatever is necessary to get rid of the recordings.

Usually, we advocate burning the records because it not only makes it impossible to get them back (or for the records to get into the hands of someone else who could be equally harmed), but also graphically demonstrates a commitment to change. Whatever means you decide to use for disposal, make certain it is permanent. Don't put your albums away in your closet, just in case you change your mind.

Remember, Jesus said, if your right hand offends you, cut it off, and if your right eye offends you, pluck it out (Matt. 5:29, 30). In other words, if there is something near and dear to you which is causing you to sin, or *could* cause you to sin, get rid of it fast.

The Bible says you best show God your love by your willingness to obey. In fact, God promises that if you demonstrate a hatred of evil by your obedience, He will bless you. Once you have gotten rid of your records, spend a little time "de-programming."

Read Scripture, or a good book. Share some time with friends and family. Once you have settled down some, you can begin to search out some good, upbuilding Christian contemporary music to fill the void left by your old rock records' demise. Don't worry, there are plenty of groups to go around and you should be able to find many artists to fit every style you enjoy.

Last, but most important of all, if you have never accepted Jesus into your life, know that He wants you to become His, that He stands ready to help you live life to the fullest, and that He loves you very much.

We have researched the subject of rock music—and in this particular book, the effects of backmasking and subliminals in rock and the media—because we're concerned about you. We want you to experience the joy Jesus can bring into your life, and we don't want anything, rock music included, to stand in the way. If you have never accepted Christ, now is the time and place. Don't delay another minute.

There's no secret formula. You simply need to ask Him to come into your life and take it over. However, if you need a little help, read over the short prayer and instructions on the following page. It will show you the way. If we can help you to become the person God wants you to be, please write us, but most of all, remember, don't settle for anything less than God's best for you.

Steps to Accepting Christ

1. Admit your need (I am a sinner). Romans 3:23: "For all have sinned, and come short of the glory of God."

2. Be willing to turn from your sins (repent). 1 John 1:9: "If we confess our sins, he is faithful and just to forgive us our sins, and to cleanse us from all unrighteousness."

3. Through prayer, invite Jesus to come in and control your life (receive Him as Savior and Lord). Romans 10:9, 10: "That if thou shalt confess with thy mouth the Lord Jesus, and shalt believe in thine heart that God hath raised him from the dead, thou shalt be saved. For with the heart man believeth unto righteousness; and with the mouth confession is made unto salvation."

What to Pray

"Dear Lord Jesus,

I know that I am a sinner and I need your forgiveness. I believe that you died on the cross for my sins. I now invite you to come into my heart and life. I want you to be the Lord (Master) of my life. Thank you, Jesus. Amen."

What's Next?

Now live for Christ with all your heart, mind and soul. Read your Bible daily. Spend time in prayer. Go faithfully to a church that preaches the gospel. And please write us and tell us what God has done for you.

Appendix 2: Congressional Subcommittee Hearings

Most Recent Findings of the Hearing Before the U.S. House Subcommittee on Transportation, Aviation, and Materials on Subliminal Communication Technology. August 6, 1984

STATEMENTS OF Dr. Hal Becker, President, Behavioral Engineering Corporation: "I believe that subliminal communications properly carried out just might be the only immediately available way to bring motor vehicle accidents, crime, and substance abuse back into manageable status.

"All three seem to be escalating, while not really responding to conventional time honored methods of treatment. And regarding Dr. Kamp's presentation, in which he said that the FCC still considers the use of subliminals deceptive, I, of course, agree with that" (p. 24).

"Both subliminal perception and hypnosis address nonconscious portions of the brain. Work by Corrigan and Becker in 1954 and 1965, 1966,

1977, 1978, Dixon, Silverman and Shevrin, have presented evidence—and many others—have presented evidence to indicate that nonconscious perception of stimuli can result in behavior change" (pp. 24, 25).

"In extensive research, Silverman has demonstrated that verbal stimuli associated with conflictual wishes have brought about behavior change" (p. 25).

STATEMENTS OF David L. Tyler, President, Proactive Systems, Inc.: (In answer to the following question: "Would [a general message] be a kind of message that could be used subliminally to get people maybe to do things that they were not otherwise interested in doing?")

"First, from our research with audio subliminals, they have to be repeated very frequently, because it is frequency and repetition that makes it effective. A brief exposure will not do much. There are other researchers that say we are wrong. It is possible that it could be done if it was appealing to some kind of emotional impact" (p. 102).

"How do you feel about regulation of subliminal communication to assure that the public is made aware of its use?"

"I don't think it should be used secretly except for crime prevention. I don't think it should be used on TV unless there is a way to verify what is there. . . . But if there is the potential for abuse, evidence of abuse, what we would recommend is legislation requiring signs be posted that subliminals are in use, and therefore there be informed consent they are there" (p. 103).

STATEMENTS OF Howard Shevrin, Ph.D., University Hospital, University of Michigan: "As a scientist, psychotherapist, and private citizen, I am quite concerned with any effort to use subliminal perception as a treatment or as a means to control behavior for commercial or any other purposes. . . . There exist sufficient grounds on which to be concerned about the public welfare in these respects" (p. 105).

"In my own work, I have shown that stimuli related to a person's emotional conflicts evoke a very different brain response subliminally (and supraliminally) than stimuli that are not emotionally disturbing for the person. . . . In other words, there is a pathological effect of subliminal messages which tune in to the person's unconscious conflicts" (p. 106).

"Let me bring some of these comments to a close by referring to an important piece of Russian research which may not be too well known in this country, which has also demonstrated that emotionally loaded words presented subliminally result in distinctive brain responses. Now, I stress this 'emotionally loaded' for several reasons, both in terms of its signficance with respect to treatment, and also with respect to the comments made earlier that indeed the shoplifter, the person who is in conflict over shoplifting, is the one who will be affected by the message, not the professional thief or the person who has no conflict over it" (p. 107).

STATEMENTS OF Lloyd H. Silverman, Ph.D., adjunct professor, New York University and research psychologist, Veteran's Adminstration, New York Regional Office: ". . . I think this is something that people don't generally recognize—that is to say, when people respond to subliminal messages even though the message may be suggestive of something, it doesn't mean that the person will either do the thing, or not do the thing. The idea that is embedded in the message, embodied by the message, could stir up something in the person that has particular meaning to him, [something] that could trigger off symptoms or intensify them.

"Now, as you implied, this could happen in everyday life and indeed it does. However, that is the chance one takes—that you have no choice about. But to be subjected to subliminal messages goes beyond one's everyday expected experience. For that reason, I think the committee is quite justified in being concerned" (p. 131).

STATEMENTS OF Maureen Ann Phillips, HPI Health Care Services, Inc.: "When subliminal communication devices are introduced, an individual's behavior is influenced or manipulated without the individual having the opportunity to immediately evaluate and think about the message that is input. Unlike other external influences, of which we are consciously aware, a subliminal message arguably bypasses our sensory mechanisms and the mechanisms by which we typically evaluate, at some level, the external input of our environment. The seriousness of this threat to individual autonomy values is, of course, measured by the level of effectiveness of subliminal communication devices.

"A very serious threat exists if such devices are capable of inducing behavior that is totally contrary to one's normal predispositions. . . . To the extent that our thinking and judgment capacities are reduced, we must consider the possibility that political and psychological freedom is simultaneously being threatened" (p. 203).

"Legal scholar and professor, Michael Shapiro, studied various behavior control techniques . . . [and] he postulates that the first amendment to our Constitution protects something that he calls 'the freedom of mentation' or the right to be free from interference with our mental processes" (p. 203).

"One eloquent description of the concerns at issue was provided by Mr. R. Schwitzgebel, in his article entitled 'Psychotechnology-Electronic Control of Mind and Behavior'. Mr. Schwitzgebel stated: 'Privacy is no more and certainly no less than the freedom of the individual to pick and choose for himself the time and circumstances under which, and most importantly, the extent to which, his attitudes, beliefs, behavior, and opinions are to be shared with or withheld from others' " (p. 203).

STATEMENTS OF Ms. Olivia Goodkin, Attorney with Goodkin, Rutter, Ebbert & O'Sullivan as found in *Southern California Law Review*, "Subliminal Communication" and presented as written testimony before the U.S. Congressional Subcommittee: "Unfortunately, undisclosed subliminal communication poses an unusual kind of captivity (the extent to which a potential audience can get away from viewing or listening to any message) since the audience cannot avert its eyes or shut its ears or retreat to private places if it does not even know that the communication is taking place. This is the highest degree of captivity of all, and such captivity undermines not only the interests such as privacy, but the principles underlying the first amendment itself. We cannot have freedom of speech and privacy if one does not know this is going on" (pp. 207, 208).

"Professor Nathaniel Branden . . . explores the impact of behavior control on autonomy. . . . He suggests that the democratic system itself is founded on the notion that people are capable of governing themselves. . . . This ability to control one's actions arises only when an individual *chooses* to focus his mind—to think. With subliminal persuasion, however, the receiver is not aware of having been influenced, nor has he consented to any such manipulation. Unaware that his thoughts or impulses are not his own, he has no reason for careful self-evaluation" (pp. 244, 245).

"When beliefs of others influence an individual's behavior without his being aware of the underlying mental activity, his psychological freedom is jeopardized, even if the subliminal communication cannot induce him to act contrary to his own predispositions. . . . The technique is capable of introducing biased information into the mind of an individual, '. . . in the form of "facts" or "judgments," that [will] later be thought of as the person's own beliefs or knowledge' " (A. Westin, *Privacy and Freedom*, 1970, p. 296).

"If subliminal techniques can influence an individual's views or behavior, his normal thought processes and censoring systems are bypassed. . . . When there is no awareness and the accompanying opportunity to think, there is no opportunity to question and judge the values implicit in the message" (p. 248).

"Attempts to control the moral content of a person's thoughts are evident in all subliminal communication techniques, regardless of the nature of the particular message" (p. 253).

"This bill was introduced May 18, 1959, [to the New Jersey State Assembly]: 'Any person who in any public place uses or permits the use by word or symbol, of a subliminal message or messages without having made immediately prior to such use a public announcement thereof and a public display of the entire body of the material to be so used is a disorderly person' " (p. 283).

"This analogy was made by the inventor of the [subliminal audio processor] device, Dr. Becker (as quoted by Art Athens, 'Beware, Here Come the Mind Manipulators,' *Family Health* magazine, December 1978, p. 40). After drawing the analogy, he said: 'What we are doing is designed to subvert something that is criminal, and let's face it, telling the whole truth isn't always the best policy' " (p. 253).

Professor Nathaniel Branden, author of *Free Will, Moral Responsibility and the Law*: "[The] social environment can provide man with incentives for good or for evil, but . . . a man's character, the degree of his rationality, independence, honesty, is determined, not by the things he perceives, but by the thinking he does or fails to do about them. . . . Of any value offered to him as the right, and any assertion offered to him as the true, a man is free to ask: *Why*? That 'Why?' is the threshold that the beliefs of others cannot cross without his consent" (pp. 276, 278).

What Does All This Mean?

As the latest overwhelming testimony of experts confirms, subliminals are being used, despite limited information as to their ultimate effects, and in spite of some frightening recent findings concerning their effects. While subliminals on rock records are, perhaps, in some ways not in the same category as many of the documented cases given before the House Subcommittee, many parallels apply, namely:

(1) Subliminals are now being proven to affect the behavior of an individual—especially one who is emotionally involved in the message. (Since the messages found on most rock records concern emotionally-charged issues for young teens such as drug use and satanic involvement, it would seem they are particularly vulnerable.)

(2) The right to protection from subliminal tampering with one's values is fully established under the law as a moral right of the individual, no matter whether the subliminal is there to sell, to inform, to persuade or simply as a joke.

(3) Subliminals appear, according to the latest findings, to be most effective when listened to repeatedly, which is the normal situation with rock music. It has been shown that the average teen listens to 6 hours of music a day—much of it repeated playings of his favorite tunes. If those tunes happen to have subliminal implants—for whatever reason—those suggestions exercise added impact.

(4) It has been discovered that people respond in different ways to the same subliminal

message; what is a perfectly innocuous statement to one individual may be an emotionally explosive trigger to another. Therefore, even the most nonsensical subliminals on rock records pose a hazard to some people. For that reason, all subliminals should either be banned or at least be noted as such on album covers.

Appendix 3: Resources

The following is a listing of source material for your own investigation of subliminal deception in both the rock music industry and in regular advertising and retail trades, as well as material on the latest documentation of rock music. Questions on the content and prices of items by Dan and Steve Peters may be sent to *Truth About Rock Ministries, P.O. Box 9222, No. St. Paul, MN 55109.*

Tapes

Backward Masking—How Subliminals Affect You by Dan and Steve Peters: Hear messages deliberately placed on rock songs, backward or through subliminal techniques. Includes comments by one of Minneapolis–St. Paul's most popular deejays, and updated information about the lyrics and lifestyles of Queen, Led Zeppelin, Cheap Trick, Electric Light Orchestra, Styx, and more. Write Truth About Rock Ministries.

Rock-A-Bye-Bye Baby (1 & 2): Hard-hitting discussions of subliminals in today's rock music.

Available from The Eagle's Nest, P.O. Box 19038, Irvine, CA 92714. Ask for tapes 205 and 206.

Books

Why Knock Rock by Dan and Steve Peters with Cher Merrill: After hundreds of hours of research and countless on-the-air debates with disc jockeys and rock stars, the authors examine not only subliminals, but both the lyrics of secular rock and the lifestyles of the rock stars themselves. Help for young people and parents in making reasoned, biblical decisions about rock music. Published by Bethany House. Available from your bookstore, or write Truth About Rock Ministries.

The Peters Brothers Hit Rock's Bottom by Dan and Steve Peters: A vivid exposé of the real world behind the false image of rock music. New, updated documentation on Billy Joel, David Bowie, Hall and Oates, Rolling Stones, Journey, BowWowWow, AC/DC, Judas Priest, and many more. Write Truth About Rock Ministries.

Documentation I—What the Devil's Wrong with Rock Music? by Dan and Steve Peters: Quotes, interviews, song lyrics and facts about rock stars, presented in new, no-nonsense form. Write Truth About Rock Ministries.

Documentation II—Rock Music Research by Dan and Steve Peters: Updated facts, figures and information on rock stars' lifestyles, lyrics, goals and graphics. Write Truth About Rock Ministries.

Backward Masking Unmasked by Jacob Aranza. Published by Huntington House, Shreveport, LA.

Rock by Bob Larson. Published by Tyndale House, Wheaton, IL.

Rock and the Church by Bob Larson. Published by Creation House, Carol Stream, IL.

Babylon Reborn by Bob Larson. Published by Creation House, Carol Stream, IL.

Media Sexploitation by Wilson Bryan Key. Published by Signet Books, New York, NY.

Clam Plate Orgy by Wilson Bryan Key. Published by Prentice-Hall, Englewood Cliffs, NJ.

The People Shapers by Vance Packard. Published by Little, Brown & Co., Boston, MA.

Articles

Art Athens, "Beware Here Come the Mind Manipulators," *Family Health* magazine (December, 1978), p. 38ff.

"Secret Voices," *Time* magazine (September 10, 1979), p. 71.

Red Flying Squirrel, "Rock in the Church," *Windstorm* magazine (October/November, 1983), p. 42.

D. H. Kehl, "Sneaky Stimuli and How to Resist Them," *Christianity Today* magazine (January 31, 1975), p. 9ff.

Vance Packard, "The New (and Still Hidden) Persuaders," *Reader's Digest* (February, 1981), p. 120ff.

Ross Pavlac, "Backward Masking: Satanic Plot or Red Herring," *Cornerstone* magazine (Volume 11: Issue 62), p. 40ff.

Richard D. Mountford, "Does the Music Make Them Do It?" *Christianity Today* (May 4, 1979), p. 21ff.

Newsletter

Truth About Rock Report: Monthly updates on the Peters Brothers' ministry, as well as in-depth, last-minute reports on the activities of secular music groups, and the latest Christian contemporary music news. Write Truth About Rock Ministries.

Films and Videos

Why Knock Rock? A one-hour video featuring the Peters Brothers in an actual seminar. Available on ½- or ¾-inch tape for sale or rental. Write Truth About Rock Ministries.

Appendix 4: Writing to Washington

A Sample Letter

Representative _____
Washington, D.C. 20515

Senator _____
Washington, D.C. 20510

Dear Congressman _____ :

It is my understanding that federal law prohibits pornography (or drug abuse) via the nation's airwaves. I recently heard a song entitled _____ on radio station _____ (give call letters). The song described (or stated) _____ . In your opinion is this pornographic (or obscene or does it promote drug use, etc.)?

I urgently request your assurance that:
(1) you are investigating the scope of this problem,
(2) you are searching for legal relief for all

120

of us and will give me details when your plans
are formulated,

(3) you are as interested as I am in insuring
a wholesome musical atmosphere for our children.

Thank you for your concern.

Sincerely,

(your name
address
city, state, zip)

A National Petition

Since our first "What the Devil's Wrong with Rock Music?" seminar in November 1979, we have been bombarded with requests for help. Parents continually ask assistance in selecting artists and records promoting positive values and morals.

We are convinced that the general trend of rock music is away from principles that build strong character, produce good citizens and unify families. We've discovered that U.S. Code Title 18, Section 1464, forbids the broadcast of obscene, indecent or profane language on public airwaves. Challenged by this, we decided it is time to ask Christians to take a stand against the playing of these pornographic records on our airwaves. Once we collect 500,000 signatures, we will hand deliver them to the President of the United States.

Please help us! If you agree rock music is having a negative effect on today's youth, join in our efforts. Feel free to make copies of the petition on page 124, then return them to us when filled. There is no age limit for this petition—just as there is no age limit on who listens to or buys pornographic rock music.

God bless!

The Peters Brothers

How to Contact the Peters Brothers

Seven countries, 40 states, 1,000 seminars, 1,000,000 attenders—the Peters Brothers will go anywhere to expose youth to the TRUTH ABOUT ROCK.

To schedule a rock music seminar in your area, have your group coordinator, pastor, youth pastor, or other interested seminar host call or write for details:

The Peters Brothers
Truth About Rock
Box 9222
North Saint Paul, MN 55109
(612) 770-8114

NATIONAL PETITION

To Stop Pornographic Music
From Being Sold to or Played on the Public Airwaves in the
Presence of Minors.

Mr. President, Members of Congress and Chairman of the F.C.C.:

We, the undersigned, are hereby petitioning all federal branches of government involved and all honorable men concerned to stop innocent children from being immorally influenced by pornography disseminated through music sold to minors or played over the public airwaves in violation of existing law which states,

"Whoever utters any obscene, indecent or profane language by means of radio communication, shall be fined not more than $10,000 or imprisoned not more than two years or both."   *U.S. Code Title 18, Section 1464*

We demand the establishment of the following:

(1) A record rating system that will aid parents in monitoring the music to which their children listen—a system similar to that used in motion picture ratings;

(2) The banning of all obscene, indecent, or profane records (or records so rated) from play over the public airwaves via radio or television;

(3) Prohibition of sale of any obscene, indecent or profane records (or records so rated) to any minor under the age of 17, except by consent of parent or guardian.

(Print address, city, state and zip)

Name				Name		
Address				Address		
City	State	Zip		City	State	Zip
Name				Name		
Address				Address		
City	State	Zip		City	State	Zip
Name				Name		
Address				Address		
City	State	Zip		City	State	Zip
Name				Name		
Address				Address		
City	State	Zip		City	State	Zip
Name				Name		
Address				Address		
City	State	Zip		City	State	Zip
Name				Name		
Address				Address		
City	State	Zip		City	State	Zip
Name				Name		
Address				Address		
City	State	Zip		City	State	Zip

Feel free to make copies of this petition. When they are filled, send to:

Truth About Rock, P.O. Box 9222, St. Paul, MN 55109.